C005

D1550138

This book is due for return on or before the last date shown below. It may be renewed by telephone, personal application, fax or post, quoting this date, author, title and the book number.

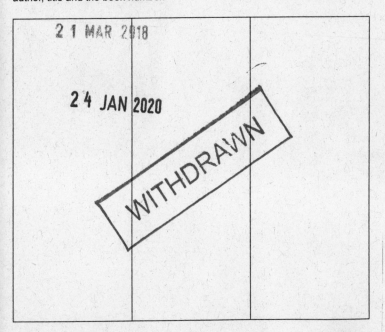

THE FLAT IN NOTTING HILL

Love and lust in the city that never sleeps!

Izzy, Tori and Poppy are living the London dream—sharing a big flat in Notting Hill, they have good jobs, wild nights out…and each other.

They couldn't be more different, but one thing is for sure: when they start falling in love they're going to be very glad they've got such good friends around to help them survive the rollercoaster…!

THE MORNING AFTER THE NIGHT BEFORE
by Nikki Logan

SLEEPING WITH THE SOLDIER
by Charlotte Phillips

YOUR BED OR MINE?
by Joss Wood

ENEMIES WITH BENEFITS
by Louisa George

Don't miss this fabulous new continuity
from Modern Tempted™!

Dear Reader

There's really nothing like the friendships created with the people you first flat-shared with when you were freshly out of home. Especially if they were also your BFFs at school.

Poppy, Tori and Izzy come from different worlds, and have different hopes and aspirations, but they get each other completely. And wherever life takes them they know they're there for each other. Even when their Notting Hill flat starts to fill up with testosterone these girls stick together.

I had a ball researching London and Notting Hill from the other side of the world in Australia, and I'm thrilled that Izzy gets to share her story with a handsome, secretive Aussie rogue.

I hope you enjoy a little workplace romance—Izzy and Harry definitely do.

May love always find you!

Nikki

THE MORNING AFTER THE NIGHT BEFORE

BY
NIKKI LOGAN

First published in Great Britain 2014
by Mills & Boon, an imprint of Harlequin (UK) Limited,
Eton House, 18-24 Paradise Road, Richmond, Surrey, TW9 1SR

© 2014 Harlequin Books S.A.

Special thanks and acknowledgement are given to Nikki Logan
for her contribution to *The Flat in Notting Hill* series.

ISBN: 978-0-263-24277-5

Nikki Logan lives next to a string of protected wetlands in Western Australia, with her long-suffering partner and a menagerie of furred, feathered and scaly mates. She studied film and theatre at university, and worked for years in advertising and film distribution before finally settling down in the wildlife industry. Her romance with nature goes way back, and she considers her life charmed, given she works with wildlife by day and writes fiction by night—the perfect way to combine her two loves.

Nikki believes that the passion and risk of falling in love are perfectly mirrored in the danger and beauty of wild places. Every romance she writes contains an element of nature, and if readers catch a waft of rich earth or the spray of wild ocean between the pages she knows her job is done.

Other Modern Tempted™ titles by Nikki Logan:

HIS UNTIL MIDNIGHT
MY BOYFRIEND AND OTHER ENEMIES
HOW TO GET OVER YOUR EX

To Louisa, Joss and Charlotte.
Thank you for a fabulous few months
living with you in Notting Hill.
First round of drinks at Ignite is on me.

PROLOGUE

WOULD SATAN WEAR eleven-micron wool?

Izzy Dean could tell, even from this side of her boss's expensive desk twelve storeys up her firm's London high-rise, that Harry Mitchell's flash charcoal suit would be as soft as a kitten to touch. Her fingers practically itched to stroke the expensive fabric.

Maybe she could cop a feel as she leaned in to smack that smug grin off his designer-stubbled face.

'Careful, Dean, you look like you want to deck me.'

'Do I?' Izzy feigned. Not that he'd believe innocence from her for one moment. He was way too used to sparring with her.

Lord, as career-enders went, wouldn't that be a spectacular way to go? Bunch up all those muscles she'd developed cleaning fast-food kitchens as a kid and—pow—set Mitchell right on his sanctimonious, perfectly sculpted arse right here in his own fishbowl office. She'd storm out amid a standing ovation from the entire downtrodden department.

'Hello?'

A large face loomed in her blurred vision and she snapped her focus back to steady blue eyes—*oasis*, according to the 'what colour are his eyes?' chart in her favourite battered old chick magazine. With flecks of *cougar blue*.

Not that she'd looked him up, specifically...*cough*

He even had eyelashes like thick, fringing palm trees to go with the whole oasis thing. Except there was nothing at all quenching about Harry Mitchell's piercing stare. Instead, it smouldered like a volcanic spring that radiated heat towards her at the most inopportune moments.

Like right now.

'You're angry.'

'And that's why you get the big bucks, Mitchell,' she sim-mered, 'that incomparable attention to detail.'

'Funny that you should mention detail—'

'There is nothing wrong with my report!'

'Not technically, no...'

She tossed her short hair back and stared him down. 'Are the numbers right?'

'You're the go-to person in the office when your colleagues can't solve something.' He glared. 'Of course they're right.'

'Then the report is fine. I see no reason to waste my time doing it again.'

He speared frustrated fingers through his hair and released a waft of something delicious and masculine into the small glass office.

Not delicious smell, she told herself. *Boss smell. Bad.*

'Is "fine" really the way you'd like to be thought of up the food chain?' he asked.

Oh, come on. 'I've worked here a lot longer than you. They know my work.'

'This work?' He held up her most recent report. 'Or this one?'

Izzy glanced at the plain folder he'd picked up with his other hand. 'What is that?'

Though her bottom lip apparently knew exactly what it was. It snuck in between her teeth and surrendered to their gentle gnaw. Mitchell's focus faltered for half a heartbeat.

But he was a fast rebounder. 'I pulled one of your reports from your first months at Broadmore Natále. It's outstanding.'

Finally! Some acknowledgement... Only twelve months in the making.

But he wasn't done. 'It's nothing like today's effort. How long do you imagine you'll be able to continue trading on your early reputation, Dean?'

She flattened her hands on his desk and leaned closer. 'I don't recall a Pulitzer Prize being in the essential criteria for this role.'

The folder hit his desk with a thud and his accent grew

more pronounced, the way it always did when he was bad-tempered. He moved around the desk to her side and glared down at her. 'Your report is flat and dull and I want to know why.'

Izzy fought hard not to let the sexy Aussie twang distract her. 'Perhaps you'd like me to write you a report on the subject?'

On that piece of comeback brilliance, she turned and slammed out of the glass door of Mitchell's office—everyone in the place had probably lip-read the entire discussion anyway—and crossed straight back to her desk, slumping into her comfy chair, where she did her best thinking.

Infinitely better than whenever she was caught up in Harry Mitchell's orbit, anyway.

Autocrat.

No one in this office was spewing out works of sublime prose in the endless reports he tasked them to produce. Maybe, once, she'd been about the technique of it all but she was all about bottom lines and pound symbols now. The facts and only the facts, because that was what got the job done and the salary paid, right?

Her shoulders slumped.

Since when was *adequate* enough for Isadora Dean? She hated that her *malaise* was clearly starting to leak through in her work but she absolutely loathed that it was Harry Mitchell calling her to attention on it.

As if he needed anything further to pick at.

She glanced around the office at all her fellow employees doing a dreadful job of pretending they weren't interested. Mitchell was right: they all brought their documents to her for a quick check over. Because she was good.

But good did not automatically equal happy.

No matter how many times you did the maths.

She flicked the little ornamental hedgehog on her desk and sent its head nodding madly. Then she snapped off the ID card pinned to her jacket and stared at it. At the bright, optimistic, enthusiastic, first-day-in-a-new-job face that stared back at her. And she remembered how she'd once felt about what she did. How grateful she was to have a good job at such a prestigious firm. How she'd totally ignored her parents' concerns when they'd replied to her emailed news. How drunk she'd got with the girls to celebrate.

What *had* happened to all that enthusiasm?

She clipped her ID card back on her jacket. Next to the hedgehog, her phone dinged to let her know she had a message. She absently flicked it open and scanned to the top.

WHEN YOU'RE THROUGH SULKING COULD YOU RETURN
SO THAT WE CAN FINISH OUR DISCUSSION, PLS?

The whole building pitched as if London were built on a fault line, and her free hand clutched the edge of her desk. But, with those few typically supercilious and irritating words, something indefinable shifted in Izzy's brain. Everything just went…left…an inch and a half, and she saw her life more clearly than she had in years.

This wasn't petulance. This was pure, unadulterated misery.

Mitchell was right. She had lost her mojo. And she didn't even notice it going.

No one wanted a lacklustre employee on their hands. Maybe she should just suck it up and go in there and promise to do better. Work on ways of getting a bit of reward back in this job.

Her phone dinged again.

She lifted her focus past her colleagues and straight to Mitchell's office. All six feet of him leaned, ankles crossed, on his desk-edge, his phone still in his hand, those blazing eyes fixed steadily on her. And, as it always did, his regard boiled her blood even as it heated less willing bits of her, too. And she realised that *this* was part of why she even bothered coming to work.

The daily zing she got from sparring with *Prince Harry* through the glass of his high-altitude corporate eyrie. Or on email. Or in team meetings.

Like a caffeine hit for her soul shooting straight through the numbness of the eight-till-six grind.

Reminding her that she was, in fact, still alive.

Part of his job involved telling her how to do hers. It wasn't personal. So why was she making it that way? Yes, he was a pain and, no, he wasn't the most supportive leader she'd ever had but it was hardly Mitchell's fault that she'd cast him as her own personal defibrillator.

For the numb days.

Maybe she could work *with* him instead of *against* him and find a happy place again deep within the relentless wheel of corporate finance.

Maybe he'd make a better ally than enemy?

But, as she stared, something in the way she was regarding him—or the reluctant acceptance he could see in her, maybe—caused three little lines to appear between his brows and he pushed away from his desk slightly, one hand half reaching towards her.

Almost beseeching.

Her gaze dropped to her phone.

BEFORE THE ICE AGE RESUMES, DEAN!

Her fingers began trembling immediately and she eased the phone onto her desk before it slipped onto the plush carpet.

So much for allies...

Then, as she sat there, seething, the most brilliant idea bloomed to life in her mind.

So brilliant, she couldn't for the life of her think why it hadn't struck earlier. She'd wasted so much time and energy.

And all the time she could be doing this!

She pushed to her feet a little unsteadily, smoothing her pencil skirt demurely down her thighs, and lifted her gaze back up to Mitchell's. Then she channelled every bit of Scarlett Johansson she could muster into the slow-motion glide over to his office and up the carpeted steps to the glass wall where he still stood, tense with irritation, and she stopped the toes of her strappy heels directly in front of his Italian leather. So they'd be touching if not for the glass divider.

She held his gaze the whole way.

Every person in the room watched her, not least Harry Mitchell, whose frustrated annoyance had been replaced by suspicious confusion. And something else. He'd watched her Scarlett-walk with incredibly satisfying interest.

Izzy wet her lips, knowing he was the only one who could see, and then leaned more closely into the glass and let her breath mist over on it.

Mitchell's voice box lurched.

She lifted her index finger to her lips and sucked it gently into her mouth, then dragged it back out down her full, moist bottom lip.

His chest rose and fell. Blue eyes remained riveted on hers. Full of the usual heat. Full of new speculation and anticipation.

And she wrote seven letters backwards in the mist on the glass.

Just two words.

One of them bad. One of them *very* bad.

Mitchell's smouldering gaze flickered down to the glass and then flared as he read her backwards statement.

'I trust that is prosaic enough for you, *sir*,' Izzy said without raising her voice.

His left brow arched high. No question that her latest written submission was unambiguous in its brevity. And no question that she was through at Broadmores regardless of whether she'd just quit.

Which she had.

She erased the misty evidence with her jacket sleeve and turned from all the sex simmering between them, ignoring the open-mouthed stares of her stunned colleagues, and crossed back to her desk on winged feet.

Three bits of scrunched-up paper tumbled out of her up-ended waste-paper basket and bounced across the floor only to be replaced with her phone, keys, hand lotion, still-nodding hedgehog and a photograph of herself, Tori and Poppy at school.

And then she just...walked out.

There was no ovation from her fellow downtrodden, and if anyone said goodbye she didn't hear it through the furious rush of blood past her eardrums.

She stepped into the lift and turned to the front, giving her a direct view of Harry Mitchell, still standing, agape, in his glass fishbowl, staring at her with a complicated mix of creases on his face.

Disappointment—the kind she was used to from her parents.

Stunned disbelief—the kind reserved for anyone who stepped off the rooftop of their career as she just had.

Loss—the kind...

She frowned. The kind she felt right now, for something she couldn't begin to understand, as the lift doors whispered shut on everything she'd thought she'd wanted from life.

CHAPTER ONE

'WHAT AM I?' Izzy murmured, wedging her shoulder and elbow in closer to the mirror propped up next to the tiny boxroom window to finish applying her mascara. 'A flipping boy wizard?'

She wouldn't mind a few magical skills if it meant she could just wave a wand to make herself beautiful in moments. Or her boobs bigger. Or her bank balance bigger. But the only part of the whole wizarding deal she had was the 'tiny room under the stairs' thing where, up until three days ago, she and her sibling flatmates had kept their miscellaneous junk.

Never mind that they were quite fancy stairs leading up to a delightful mezzanine floor she'd once adored. Never mind that it had, in fact, been an *actual* room before it was their boxroom. It was unquestionably tiny.

A poor girl's room.

Bad enough that she'd had to ship most of her belongings to her parents' council house back in Chorlton, but her impulsiveness had put everyone out because Poppy and Alex had to relocate their thirds of the overflow, too, and couldn't move it into Izzy's old room because that now needed to be let to meet the repayments.

Sigh. Her room… Her beautiful room.

Someone else's soon.

She swapped the mascara to the other hand and tried for a better result from the left.

'The price of freedom,' she reminded herself aloud.

And of self-respect. Everything she'd done in her life was about treating herself with more respect than the world had ever treated her.

'Izzy…' Poppy rapped on the door then stuck her head in, skilfully avoiding taking an eye out on the various clothes hangers hooked over the door frame. 'How much of your own party are you planning on missing?'

Was *all of it* a wise thing to admit?

She normally loved a party, loved being the centre of attention—she had a lifetime of non-existent parties to make up for—but *Congrats, you're unemployed* was not her preferred theme. Even if Poppy had typically gone with the more positive, *Congrats, you're out of the job that was draining your soul.* There certainly was something to be said for spin. Izzy pushed back from the ridiculously ornate dresser wedged awkwardly between the wall and the single bed.

Single...

This was what she'd become—a half made-up pauper sleeping on a child's bed.

The price of freedom.

'Did I hear Tori's laugh?' Izzy quizzed, brightly. And by 'laugh' she meant the carillon of flirtatious bells that was their best friend's weapon of choice. 'How long has she been here?'

Poppy arched a single, elegant brow. 'I think the more pertinent question is how long have *you* been in here? It's just gone eight.'

'Oh.'

The boxroom was too crowded for a clock and Izzy never wore a watch. 'Time to come out, then.'

Why on earth had she thought being unemployed was worth celebrating?

Because that decision had been made two days ago. Today she'd changed her mind. Two days from now she'd probably feel differently again. Par for the course with her wildly swinging thoughts lately.

Wildly swinging, dissatisfied thoughts.

So dissatisfied that she'd even considered ringing her mum to talk things through. Until she remembered that she didn't do that anymore.

'Come on, Iz,' Poppy urged, reading her expression and holding the door wide. 'You'll enjoy it once you get out there.'

She certainly wouldn't without a champers in hand. One

look at the thronging mass in their flat reinforced that. All friends, but somehow still overwhelming. Would it be rude to go to a movie instead? To reward the kindness of all their friends who'd rallied for her with her absence?

She paused in the doorway. They wouldn't be the first kind people she'd abandoned.

But tonight was not the night to be thinking about her parents or her dysfunctional childhood. Tonight was a night for stoic smiles and fellowship.

She followed Poppy into the kitchen, keeping her eyes down until she had the familiar comfort of a glass in her hand. 'Please tell me there's Lanson.'

'Dunno. Brother dearest ordered the booze.'

There was—thank God—and Izzy polished off her first glass while rinsing the used party glasses already accumulating in the kitchen. She took care of a second while chopping up a platter of out-of-season veg.

Their extended circle of friends fell like Brighton seagulls onto her choppings.

'God, I love this stuff,' a tall brunette cooed, scooping a big dollop of dip onto some capsicum and then shoving the lot into her mouth and speaking past the crunching mess. 'Yours?'

'Speciality of the man of the house,' Izzy said. And, no, dip wasn't an odd thing for a military man to be good at. No more odd than Alex's weirdly nocturnal habits, anyway.

'Tash, Sally.' She nodded, extending the platter for their grazing pleasure. 'Thanks for coming. Hi, Richard.'

'Love the pauper's catering, Izzy,' he gushed, drowning a sprig of broccolini in dip. 'Very on-theme.'

Huh. If being poor was so entertaining why hadn't she smiled more as a kid?

She shuffled forwards through the crammed-in guests, keeping herself and the veg creeping steadily towards the far side of the bright, eclectically decorated industrial conversion. Guests greeted and commiserated and dipped the whole way.

'So what's next?' one of her downstairs neighbours shouted over the music and chatter.

'Not sure,' Izzy hedged. 'Consolidation period?'

The pretty face folded. 'Oh, I assumed you had something already lined up.'

Nope. Not a thing lined up. Though reasonable that her friends would expect that, because that was absolutely what normal Izzy would do. The Izzy they all knew.

Corporate, clever Izzy.

Top of the class and best in her department Izzy.

But new Izzy, it seemed, was channelling her mother, all of a sudden. Choosing *principle* over *plenty*. New Izzy was all about the moment and dramatic, flourishing statements. And nothing about reality.

She paused against one of the apartment's large windows and caught her breath ready for another pass with the half-decimated tray. The sea of people momentarily parted and she caught a glimpse of Tori's distinctive tri-coloured hair. She was perched happily in a man's lap, her 'take me' heels kicked back, his strong hands the only thing stopping her from toppling backwards onto the floor in front of all their friends. Not her boyfriend's slim, pale, slightly creepy hands. These were strong, tanned, non-Mark hands.

Uh-oh…trouble in paradise? Already?

The throng closed in once more, ending her worrying Tori sighting, and Izzy pressed on with her vegetables back towards the kitchen. Appeasing the masses.

Ooh…perhaps waitressing could be her new job. Apparently she had a knack for it and maybe the café down on street level would hire her, then she'd have no commute costs. Of course there was the whole issue of zero appreciable waiting skills.

The only after-school job she'd managed never to have in her long, exhausting childhood.

The final stick of courgette disappeared just before Izzy hit the kitchen doors. Of course it did. Because she'd cut just enough for the size of the crowd she'd unconsciously counted, and she'd shuffled forward in subliminal accordance with the diminishing supply.

Quantities. Numbers. They were her thing. Estimates and value assessment and principles of return. Whether it was Broadmore Natále's investments or a pile of crunchy veg, the theory was much the same. Leverage all available resources and minimise waste.

Yawn.

No wonder she'd left. Her job gave her a fantastic income and that gave her a fantastic, inner-city lifestyle, but there wasn't much else to recommend it. Not the fiddly commute, not the irritating, God's gift boss, not the groundhog-day workload.

Job security just wasn't enough anymore. Who had she been kidding convincing herself that achieving *budget* was the kind of professional achievement she'd been craving her whole life?

Sigh.

She dumped the empty tray into the sink and reached for the chopping knife.

When he'd set out tonight to get his way with a woman it wasn't *this* woman he'd had in mind. And not this kind of *way*, either.

Still, Harry considered as he flattened his palm against the firm ass presently resident in his lap, things could definitely be worse. Maybe he could indulge Matahari, here, just ten more minutes. Spend a bit of time with a flesh-and-blood woman.

One who was happy to see him.

Plus, he didn't know anyone here and he was grateful for the smokescreen while he carried out essential reconnaissance on Izzy Dean.

Isadora.

He'd almost pity her that if he weren't so angry at being here.

A diva didn't get any less diva-ish just because she was good at her job. Or good to look at. And she was, in a lanky, Keira Knightley kind of way. The glass walls of his office had given him plenty of opportunity to conduct an assessment when she was otherwise engaged. Or when she wasn't. And he'd used them to the fullest.

He'd been grooming Dean to replace him when he moved on at the end of his stint, but after Wednesday's spectacular meltdown...

Let her walk.

The firm could well do without high-maintenance attention seekers.

Yet here he was, cap in bloody hand, sent to persuade her to reconsider, because she'd walked on his watch. Which apparently made getting her back his responsibility.

The tense anger of Broadmore's human resources director, Rifkin, yesterday afternoon echoed back at him. Implying, but never saying outright, that Dean's hasty departure was somehow his fault. As if her inability to accept constructive criticism and cede to authority weren't the bulk of the problem. He'd argued that, but Rifkin had challenged him with a list of staff they'd lost since he'd come aboard and asked how they could *all* develop such terminal flaws after years of working together well.

Implication: his fault.

Harry's interpretation: dead wood, well rid of.

Just because someone had been around for a while didn't mean they were still adding value.

Even if she was the most talented person on his team.

Then again Rifkin hadn't seen the words on the glass of his office wall...

'Eyes forward, handsome,' the vixen in his lap purred as if he'd been checking out her rack, not her friend serving celery sticks to the ravenous hordes. He dragged his focus reluctantly back to her eyes, which were more than a little liquor-glazed.

He was definitely off his game.

'Are you sure you're not uncomfortable?' he tried, again.

'No, I'm great.' She wiggled her butt down further, which only served to make him significantly less comfortable.

A tiny brunette flopped down into the empty half-space next to them. Not quite big enough for her, leaving her pressed closely to him and, for half a moment, he feared his troubles had just doubled.

But then her eyes filled with casual sparkle and she leaned around him and said, 'All right, Tori?'

Tori. That was what she'd mumbled while he was busy staring at Izzy Dean. And the little brunette was not a flanking assault; she was the extremely welcome cavalry.

'Fantastic, Poppy.' Tori waved her friend's concern away with dramatic sweeps. 'Having a great time. Have you met Harry?'

The brunette thrust out her hand. 'Hello, Poppy Spencer. This is my flat.'

Which was pretty much polite social code for 'who are you and who invited you?' Just because he'd been out of the scene for a few years didn't mean he'd forgotten the rules. Shaking Poppy's hand was the perfect excuse to ease Tori into a slightly more upright and appropriate position without causing offence.

'Nice to meet you,' Harry hedged, unwilling to give away too much. 'So this is your party?'

'My flatmate's actually. She's just out of a dreadful job.'

'Do you always celebrate employment changes?'

'This one we do. Izzy's been miserable for months. Lousy job, lousy new boss. She's well out of it.'

Lousy?

'Maybe a job is what you make it,' Harry defended.

'She made that one long enough.' Tori pouted prettily. 'You can't polish a turd.'

To have his entire career aspiration and management expertise summarily written off stung. Like a bitch.

'Would you like a drink, Harry?' Poppy offered, though he wasn't sure how she thought he would manage a glass with both hands full of busty, wriggling woman.

'I'd love one,' he said. 'And I wouldn't mind meeting your flatmate. Congratulate her on her…new-found freedom.'

Drag her back to the firm kicking and screaming, if necessary.

'Conveniently they're in the same place. Izzy's hiding in the kitchen.'

Hiding? That wasn't the woman he knew. Isadora Dean was always the centre of attention in any space. Laughing and shaking back her dark blond mop and generally being delightful to her adoring audience.

And thoroughly distracting to him.

She should have been in her element at a party that was all about her.

He set Tori to her feet and she happily took him by his loosened tie and led him through the crowd to the kitchen.

'Izzy,' she gushed dramatically, entering with him and Poppy in tow. 'A man without a drink is a tragedy not to be borne.'

The woman in question emerged from behind the fridge door, a warm smile on her face, and turned automatically to the sink full of ice and beer. But the smile died the moment she saw who stood in her kitchen.

'What the bloody hell are you doing here?'

'Izzy!' Poppy's shock could have been for the language as much as the tone.

'Dean.' He nodded, cautiously.

'What is he *doing here?*' she hissed again, as if he weren't in the room. Kind of desperately.

'He's a guest...' Tory squinted, then twisted to look at him. 'Isn't he?'

'He's my boss!' Dean sputtered.

Tori dropped his tie and it fell, flaccid, against his suit. Both women turned on him and there was a surprising amount of unity in the three angry female faces now facing him.

'*Ex*-boss,' he reminded her. Though hopefully not for long. He thrust his hand out to finish the introductions Poppy had started. 'Harry Mitchell.'

'You're really him?' Poppy squeaked.

'But you're gorgeous,' Tori helpfully contributed. 'I imagined you hideous and old.'

Dean's face flamed. 'Tori! Bad enough you've been giving him a lap dance—'

She rolled her eyes. 'I didn't know, Iz. Obviously.'

Dean reached for her glass and clutched it, white-knuckled, like a weapon. 'Why are you here?'

'To see you.'

'I hope you're not planning on begging her to come back.' Poppy laughed. 'You could have saved yourself the tube fare.'

Begging. Cajoling. Bribing. Little Miss Potty-Mouth had suddenly become Britain's most wanted. As galling as that was.

'There was an email circulating, inviting all staff.' He shrugged. 'I'm staff.'

'You're not staff, you're my supervisor,' Dean pointed out. He took a shred of comfort from her use of the present tense.

'Management weren't excluded,' he thrust. As if staff communiques usually came with small print.

'So, now even my party invites are sub-standard?' she parried. 'Common decency excludes you.'

Yeah, *this* was more the Isadora Dean he recognised. Uptight and defensive. And all pink and breathless when she was riled. Which he took care to do often. 'Well, I'm here now.'

'You're not welcome,' she pointed out, as if there was any question at all. And not the rudest thing she'd ever said to him. His memory filled with her offensive departure and then overflowed with the memory of those lips sucking on her finger.

He cleared his throat.

'Could be worse. At least I'm not moving in.'

Dean blinked at him. 'What?'

'There's a guy out there with two full duffel bags. At least you know I'm only here for a few hours.'

Poppy's face creased. 'Out there?'

He cast her a sideways look. Gentler, because he quite liked her and she'd genuinely tried to save him from Matahari earlier. 'Go see for yourself.'

Poppy threw Dean an apologetic look and then excused

herself, the party noise surging until the doors swung shut again as she stomped through.

One down, one to go. He needed Dean alone for this conversation. If he was going to demean himself it wouldn't be with an audience.

'He was pretty buff, too,' he added casually, looking right at Tori.

To her credit she stood firm. For about four seconds. Then...

'Sorry, Iz,' she whispered before hastening out after Poppy.

Dean's eyes darkened even further when his returned to her. 'This is my home, Mr Mitchell.'

'Harry.'

The indignation on her face did what it usually did to him and stirred around in places he tried not to disturb. Righteousness leaked out of her like wayward passion.

'You weren't invited.'

'I hardly broke in. The downstairs door was wedged open. I think the law would back me on this one.'

'Employee harassment laws might not.'

'You're not my employee.' Not currently. The only reason he was letting his hormones off the chain just a little.

She grabbed the champagne bottle and refilled her glass, spilling it over in her haste. Liquid gold ran down her long, expressive fingers where she clutched the glass stem. 'You truly expect me to believe that you were so bereft of something to do on a Friday night in London that you came along to the farewell party of an employee who'd just told you to—'

'Careful, Dean. Do you really want to say it twice?'

Her anger subsided like the fizz in her champagne. 'Why are you here?'

'Isadora, how can we improve if we get no feedback?' he asked reasonably.

'Izzy!' she gasped. 'No one calls me Isadora.'

'It's on your file.'

'But that doesn't mean I like to be called it.'

And, just like that, he had her permission to call her by her familiar name, and hostilities between them cranked down a notch. Though not so far that he didn't make a mental note for later to poke around a bit in the sore spot he'd just uncovered.

'Fair enough. Izzy. If you call me Harry.'

'I won't be calling you anything for much longer. You're not staying.'

'I've not had my drink yet.'

She glared at him. 'If I get you a drink, you'll leave?'

'Probably. I just let my strongest chance of hooking up walk out the door, after all.'

His dig had exactly the right effect. Izzy flashed fire again. 'She is nobody's hook-up. Tori is in a relationship, actually.'

'Could have fooled me,' he shot back.

She passed him an open beer as though it were a grenade. Icy cold, as a beer should be.

'Interesting place,' he finally said, swallowing down his umbrage with the amber nectar. He had a job to do and he wasn't going to achieve it while she was still angry. That was why she'd quit in the first place.

'We like it.'

Okay, not giving an inch. 'Old factory?'

She took a long, deep breath and seemed to finally realise how rude she was being. Even if he wasn't quite a guest. 'Fire station. We have the top floor and turret. There are several smaller flats downstairs and the café down on the street.'

Oh, so grudging. And he'd be damned if he'd let her do that to him. So he started poking.

'You have a turret?'

'It's my bedroom.' Then her pale skin forked between her eyes. 'Used to be.'

He opened his mouth to reply but she cut him off. 'That is not an invitation.'

'I'm very happy with my place overlooking the Thames, actually.'

Her hair swung in silky pieces around her angular jaw. 'Swanky river view; why does that not surprise me?'

'Why is it swanky to overlook water?'

'It's just such a cliché.'

He let that one through to the keeper. Better than admitting he needed the sounds and smells of the water splashing the sides of the embankment to keep himself sane. Awkward silence fell again.

'How are you enjoying the sleep-ins?' he finally ventured.

'All two of them? Lovely. I could get used to it.'

Just part of what baffled him about Izzy Dean: apparently miserable in her job yet a work ethic strong enough to have her at her desk before everyone else arrived. Brilliant operator until the day she just…stopped trying.

He leaned one hip on the kitchen island and kept his voice as casual as he could so she wouldn't remember that he'd virtually promised to leave when she gave him his beer. 'When do you start your new job?'

Her pupils flared enough to see from across the island. 'Not…immediately. I'm looking forward to some time off.'

'Nice for some.'

'Please…' The word bloomed mist on the edge of her glass as she took a sip. His whole body tightened at the reminder of her spectacular performance in the office. 'You can't tell me your management salary doesn't buy you whatever leisure time you want.'

'Not if I want to keep making that salary,' he muttered. 'I haven't had a decent break in five years.'

That, at least, was true. He spent nearly as much time at home researching the business as he did in the office delivering it. Downtime was lost time in his book.

'Well, that explains a lot.'

'Such as?'

'Perhaps if you had a holiday now and again you would be a little easier to work with.'

With champagne came courage, apparently.

'You think *I'm* hard to work with?'

She didn't miss his emphasis. 'I do, actually. I'm more of a *more flies from honey* kind of person.'

Yeah. He'd bet. Pretty much anything to do with honey fitted Isadora Dean. Her skin tone, her voice. His eyes drifted straight to her lips.

Honey. Definitely.

'You think a manager should be nice to his staff, all the time?' he said, to distract himself from that line of thought.

'I think a working relationship is a partnership, not a tyranny.'

'A partnership in which *I* pay *you* to work.'

'Just think how much more productive I'd be if I was interested in earning your respect.'

Ouch.

But he at least took some solace from her use of the present tense. Maybe this whole thing was just a ploy for more money from an ambitious employee. Effective: he was authorised to up her pay packet by ten grand.

'I have thirty-three direct reports in this role. Not too sustainable to be buddy-buddy with each of them.'

Especially not when he kept finding reasons to haul a particularly sexy and recalcitrant one into his office.

'Boohoo.' She tossed back the last of her champagne. 'Anyway, officially not my problem since I'm not your employee anymore and never will be.'

He shifted closer. And he liked it. He'd never allowed himself to get this close to her before. Too dangerous.

'Never?'

She stood her ground. 'Nope.'

'You have no price that you'll eventually come to after a day or two of faux deliberation?'

Insult blazed heavily in her pretty eyes. 'Nope.'

She pressed her hand to her breast and all it did was remind him she had them. His eyes went straight to those long, champagne-sticky fingers pressed against her blouse and the slight curve beneath. But he fought it.

'Everyone has a price.'

'Is that why you're here?' She gaped. 'To see what it will cost you to get me back?'

He wasn't about to let her start thinking that she was special. 'We invest a lot in our staff. I don't like to see anyone walk away with that investment. Or our corporate knowledge.'

'I signed your confidentiality agreement. Broadmore Natále's secrets are safe with me.'

Actually, he believed her. She might be a princess but she'd always been a discreet and professional princess. Wednesday excepted. And peering up at him as she was—all enormous-eyed and unflinching—she certainly looked very sincere.

And he was through begging.

Rifkin be damned.

'I told them you'd tell me to go to hell.'

Realisation dawned in her eyes. And with it, a hot little smile. 'Oh, I see… You've been *sent*.'

He just glared.

She shifted onto one hip and the move changed the angle of the classy outfit she was wearing, highlighting the line of her body. 'That must really pain you.'

You have no idea.

'I gave it a shot,' he breathed. 'I need to get your keycard back, then.'

All warmth from their sparring drained from her eyes like the dregs from her glass. 'Security can't just disable it?'

'They're ten-quid access cards.'

She flushed and actually looked a little hurt that he didn't even consider her worth ten pounds.

Really? That was her hot button—devaluing her? Handy to know.

'Whatever. Follow me.'

The sudden distance she put between them was almost like a cool chill after the warmth of their heated discussion. Exactly when had it stopped being business and started being flirting? He took one final tug on his beer then left the three-quarters-full bottle on the kitchen bench and trailed her back out through the doors, being sure to appreciate the round sway of her arse.

Now that he could.

CHAPTER TWO

'WATCH YOURSELF,' IZZY murmured exactly as her ex-boss ducked sideways and down to avoid clipping his egotistically big head on the steel frame of the mezzanine stairs going up to the bedroom above them. Though a scar would probably only make him more handsome.

She shoved her shoulder against her door.

'You're kidding me,' he said over the party music. 'This is you?'

Spinning revealed him to be much closer than she'd expected. And it only served to remind her how tiny her new room really was. And how chaotic.

'Much as I'd like to lock you in the store room as a hilarious prank and listen to you beating at the door while no one else could hear you, I do, in fact, need to sleep in here tonight. So I'll just find my ID card and you can be on your way.'

'What happened to the turret?'

Why did he look so concerned? 'Poppy's renting it to someone else.'

'Your best friend evicted you?'

'God, no. She'd never ask that. I swapped rooms. Economies of scale.'

'Economical is right,' he murmured. 'I have a linen closet bigger than this.'

She smiled tightly. 'Are you always so gracious?'

Colour streaked up his jaw and it confused her as much as a rare trace of humility in him always did. 'I just… It doesn't fit.'

'Nothing fits, as you can see.'

He dragged his gaze the very short distance from the left of the room to the right, taking in her pathetic bed and her mounded-up belongings. 'Is this because you quit the firm?'

Something about the size of him in her tiny room, the male

scent swilling into every corner, the sexy accent and maybe the multiple champagnes in quick succession stole all but the most essential air from her lungs. But not so much that she couldn't protest his monumental ego.

'The world does not revolve around you, Harry Mitchell, surprising as that may be.'

'So you chose to live like this because...?'

'Because I'm careful with my money.' Oh, such lies. 'And because it's easier for Poppy to rent the best room than this one.'

It had nothing at all to do with the fact that despite earning stupid money for the past few years she'd actually managed to put very little of it away for the rainy day that had now come. That she'd gone a bit spend-mad with the first real money she'd ever had at her disposal and then become ridiculously accustomed to it. Reliant on it. Which made the myriad belongings cluttered around them now very quality belongings...but still clutter.

And not the gently shambolic clutter of her parents' meagre belongings. The clutter of someone with a life rapidly outgrowing her circumstances.

Much like her ambition.

She'd always had a disconnection between what she wanted and what life had given her. The only girl in her childhood estate with big-city ambitions.

Many people might call it denial.

Behind her, Harry leaned on the wall while she began the hunt for her work ID card. It wasn't in the pile she'd hastily thrown together at her desk. No, that was because she'd been wearing it that day.

Her jacket... Where was Wednesday's jacket?

She turned back for the door and paused in front of his inconvenient bulk.

'Excuse me.'

Harry straightened and she squeezed past, the back of her calves pressing against her bed and her front brushing against the expensive fabric of his open coat. His lips twisted as he stretched taller to give her space and politely focused over her head on a point across the small room. Izzy rummaged around in the clothes hanging on the back of the door they'd just come through until she found the cropped jersey jacket she'd worn on Wednesday, and unclipped the security tag still pinned to its lapel.

'There you go.' She pressed it into his front as she squeezed past again.

His fingers automatically came up to catch it before she dropped it, but they snagged hers instead, pressing them into his not inconsiderable chest.

Izzy froze. Hard heat soaked through his cotton shirt and charred her skin.

'Seriously,' he urged as her eyes flashed up to him, his fingers still holding hers captive, 'reconsider.'

His voice had dropped down somewhere much more gravelly and, down there, his accent did its best work.

'Seriously,' she mimicked. 'I don't go back on my decisions.'

'Ever?'

'Ever.'

'Even the bad ones?'

'Especially the bad ones. There's no going back from those, only forwards.' And she knew that from experience.

She glanced up into his fathomless eyes and heard her next words tumble from her lips. Surprised even herself with her candour. 'That job was killing me. It was time. Regardless of everything else.'

'You've only been in it for a couple of years.'

'It's not boredom. It's—' *me!* '—the work.'

'So, go for a different job within the firm.'

She suddenly became aware that her fingers still pressed into his pectoral region and she tugged them gently free and curled them at her side. 'What is it to you? Why do you even care?'

'Because you were a good employee,' he murmured down at her, all smoky intensity. 'My best.'

Pfff. 'We fought every day.'

He slipped his hands into his trouser pockets and the move effectively pushed him out from the wall and a smidge closer to her. She didn't step back. On principle. This was *her* domain, tiny as it might be. The scented heat pumping off him pleasantly consumed her.

'You challenged me every day,' he corrected.

It felt odd testing him now, standing this close and peering up at him. Hardly a position of power. Yet she felt as if the cards were all hers. 'You made some bad decisions.'

It was only when his lips twisted so fully that she remembered what a nice mouth he had. When it wasn't issuing ridiculous demands.

'Clearly you thought so. But they were my decisions to make.'

'If you just want a bunch of yes-men in your department then why are you here, trying to get me back?'

'Because diversity is apparently healthy in a workforce—'

'Not if it's only token.'

'—and because, surprising as it might seem, I appreciate spirit in women.'

'Like horses?' She snorted.

He wisely ignored that. 'Spirit and brains.'

'Uh-huh. So all those times you and I ended up locking horns, that was…*appreciation* making you flush red?'

He did it again now and it added a dangerous kind of gleam to his eyes.

'You tell me.'

She crossed her arms angrily and it only served to plump her minor cleavage up a tad in the aperture of her blouse when viewed from virtually above. Which, naturally, he took full advantage of. Izzy dropped her hands by her side, instead, to take away his toy. It left his eyes nowhere to go but back to hers, all simmering and smart and way, *way* too close.

'Come on, Dean,' he purred, 'you can't say our…discussions didn't give the daily grind a productive boost.'

There were times she'd have liked to have *boosted* Harry

Mitchell right out of his twelfth-floor window. 'Strange as it may seem to you, my productivity goes up when I'm re-spected professionally.'

His eyebrows shot up. 'You think I don't respect you?'

'You don't respect my opinion. Anyone's really.'

'Disagreeing with it and not respecting it aren't the same thing. Anyway, occasionally I did agree with you.'

She knew. And weren't those days the most confusing of all? Because he did so unconditionally. And wholeheartedly. She bit her lip and his gaze went straight to the childhood gesture.

'You know what I'm starting to think?' he murmured, still checking out the nibble of her teeth on her lips.

'Enlighten me.'

'Maybe all our fighting was just sexual tension in disguise.'

The room was way too small for her bark of a laugh. It fairly ricocheted off the walls. 'You must be joking.'

'Not at all.' He grinned and it was the most predatory she'd ever seen from him. And smug.

'Because you're so irresistible?'

'Because we have chemistry. I thought it was just me but Wednesday put a big question mark over that.'

No, they didn't. Not chemistry and not Harry Mitchell. Hot or not. 'Maybe you're just projecting your own hormones.'

'You don't feel it?'

Challenge, not question. As if he already knew the answer. As if she did, too. But they bred them tough in Manchester. She tossed her short hair back. 'Not particularly.'

Liar, liar...

'February twenty-first this year,' he challenged. 'We shared the same lift and the end-of-day rush pushed us together at the back. We didn't speak a word to each other and the only uncovered parts of us touching were our ungloved hands.' He stepped a tiny bit closer. 'But we both walked out of the building rubbing the tingles away.'

'No, we—'

'April third.' He lifted his chin. 'I knocked back one of

your ideas and you spent a good portion of the day glaring at me through the walls—all flushed and infuriated and eyes spitting—and I spent a good portion of the day with half a hard-on, as a result.'

No way her gasp should have caught quite that tightly in her chest. She should have been outraged, not breathless.

Not excited.

Her glares across her crowded open-plan office to his lofty glassed-in one *had* simmered, and not always with anger. She'd felt it but had no idea he'd been able to see it.

God...

'You're making these up.'

'Check your diary,' he dismissed, plunging his hands even deeper in his pockets. 'June eleventh, just before lunch. You stood in my office giving me hell about the new ratios and I just let you run because I was curious.'

She swallowed back a lump of dread. She remembered June eleventh. The room had been practically soaked with awareness and she'd come away fairly throbbing from the argument. And then she'd beaten herself up all day about the inappropriateness of it all. He was her boss. He was the *bad guy.*

Words formed themselves despite her best intentions.

'Curious about what?' she croaked.

His lips twisted. 'Have you never heard the saying that a person fights like they f—?'

'Stop!' Air sucked hard into her lungs and then froze there, trapped, making it harder to squeeze out, 'I thought that was dancing.'

'I found June eleventh extremely illuminating on that front. But nowhere near as illuminating as Wednesday. Wednesday was a real eye-opener.'

Her only hope of salvation here was in channelling a bit of Tori's hearty sexual confidence. She tossed her hair back and met his eyes directly.

'You never let on.'

'Of course not. It wasn't appropriate.'

Hysteria bubbled dangerously close. 'And this is?'

'You're not exactly moving away from me.'

She glanced at the junk all around them. 'That's more a statement about my hoarding than your hotness.'

Crap. Not what she'd meant to say. At all.

His left eyebrow lifted. 'I'm hot?'

'You're insufferable.' That smug grin sure was.

'You think I'm attractive.'

'I think you're dangerously close to a lawsuit.'

His laugh echoed her earlier bark. 'For what?'

'Employee sexual harassment.'

He waggled her ID tag. 'You quit, remember?'

'Then, sexual harassment just generally.'

He shuffled closer. 'You still haven't asked me to leave. That's all it will take.'

No. Why was that…?

'Maybe I'm hoping chivalry isn't dead.' Maybe, deep down inside, she wanted to give him one more chance to be a decent man.

'Grand chivalric gestures were the only outlet for all the unrequited sexual frustration in the twelfth century.' He shot her his best Cheshire grin. 'Like our fighting.'

'Well, then, perhaps your grand gesture could involve sweeping heroically out the door and nicking off.'

His smile this time was half laugh. And it was annoyingly appealing. 'Or we could find a more traditional outlet for all the tension.'

'No.' It would be laughable if the very thought hadn't divested her of the oxygen she'd need to do it.

'Are you already in a relationship?' he challenged. 'I'm not.'

Izzy grasped desperately at the edges of the conversation. Harry's eyes said he was dead serious, but how could he be? This sort of thing never happened to her. Despite her best efforts.

She sucked in some much-needed air. 'Except with your career.'

His eyes dimmed oh-so-briefly. 'My career and I have an understanding.'

'When it gets you laid?'

'Is that what you think this is about?' He looked genuinely wounded. 'Sex?'

Doubt crept in at the corners. 'Unless you're proposing a rollicking game of chess?'

'Something tells me you'd be quite good at chess,' he murmured. 'I'm talking about exploration. A bit of good old-fashioned groping. Tangling tongues and heavy breathing. When was the last time you had that?'

Ah…no. Not a question she was going to answer. 'You're assuming rather a lot, don't you think?'

'You still haven't asked me to leave.'

The simple truth of that stripped Izzy bare. He was flirting and she was, too, in her own clunky way. They were standing in a darkened, tiny bedroom close enough to get right into that groping without even needing to reach. They no longer had any kind of professional relationship to protect or reputation to preserve. She knew him well enough to know he wasn't some kind of weirdo or monster. And there *was* a strange kind of hormonal haze going on thanks to the intriguing fingertip preview of the hard body under his McQueen business shirt.

He was offering her a few hours of healthy distraction and making it clear that it didn't have to end in sex and, most importantly, he was exactly the right kind of guy for a one-night-only appearance.

And she wasn't throwing him out.

'A good time but not a long time? Is that it?' she murmured.

'A *great* time, Izzy,' he clarified, 'but no…not a long time.'

Yes, yes, yes, her three champagnes ganged up to whisper violently in her ear. But everyone knew champagne was a tart.

'Because you have your career?'

'Because I'm not looking for a relationship.'

'But you're open to a fun night.'

'That's up to you, Iz.'

Iz…

That one diminutive sealed her fate, seducing her with its simple masculinity and emboldening her with its intimacy.

That one diminutive made it easier to imagine—to stick her fingers in her ears and go *la la la* for a few hours—that they knew each other even vaguely well enough for what he was proposing. For what she suddenly realised she was contemplating.

And was desperately, obscenely hungry for. And maybe always had been.

What was there to know? He was gorgeous, he was Australian, he smelled like a god. What if he kissed like one, too? And what if she never found out, first hand? And she wouldn't because, without turning up in his building at eight every morning, this was the last she was ever going to see of infuriating Harry Mitchell.

Intriguingly sexy Harry Mitchell.

Maybe he was right about their office bickering, maybe it was just the only work-appropriate way for the chemistry to get out.

Because she could sure feel it now, surging like a tidal current between them, urging her closer, urging her to say yes. Urging her to give in to the speculative curiosity she suddenly realised she'd always had about him.

'Can I touch your suit?' she asked, eyes not quite meeting his. Not believing she'd asked.

'My...suit?'

She ignored his rich chuckle and stretched her fingers towards the same jacket he'd been wearing on Wednesday. He stood perfectly still as they feathered down onto the curve of his shoulder and even stiller when she flattened them against his breast.

Her suspended breath released on a strangled half groan. 'It's beautiful.'

Those blue eyes narrowed suspiciously. 'Did you just climax?'

'I wanted to do this on Wednesday,' she confessed, smiling.

'Well, you're in luck. You can do whatever you want to me tonight.'

Whatever you want...

Her fingers curled back into a fist of their own volition and she reluctantly lowered it.

'This is awkward,' she whispered, all truth. Because she'd never, ever done the one-night stand thing. 'I don't know what to do.'

'Tell me to leave. Or step forward. Or touch my suit again.' His shrug was the merest shoulder flick. 'Totally up to you.'

Ugh…

She'd wanted chivalry but now that she had it she really wanted him to sweep her up into his arms in the boorish manner he usually conducted himself in and take the choice away from her. The responsibility. But his apparent ambivalence wiggled in under her carefully erected self-confidence and poked uncomfortably at the place where all her old insecurities still lived. Shouldn't he be gagging to kiss her? Wouldn't that be more romantic? The fact he wasn't triggered her old insecurities—thoughts of every boy at school who preferred the racier girls, the prettier girls.

The cleaner girls.

*Isadora couldn't be poorer…*the old voices echoed.

Except she didn't feel poor tonight. She felt obscenely rich with opportunity. And, despite his nonchalance, Harry's heartbeat under her fingertips just now hadn't thumped as if she wasn't good enough.

She locked eyes with his and stepped forward into his body, then linked her hands behind his head.

'When I imagined wrapping my hands around your neck,' she whispered, 'this wasn't quite what I had in mind.'

Now, that muscular neck was a convenient place for her to hook herself—like any of the fine outfits dangling from hangers around her new room—so that her lips were more levelly placed with his.

The surprise in his eyes was swiftly succeeded by masculine anticipation. His perfectly manicured hands slipped straight up to her ribs and bonded there.

And his lips met her more than halfway.

Soft flesh met its mate. Tongue touched on teeth. Large

hands slid over her body—one up below her breast, its friend around and over the curve of her bottom—as his mouth plundered hers.

Thoroughly.

Indecently.

And she realised that all those secret glances she'd cast at his sexy mouth were shamefully under-informed about his talents. Of course he was a good kisser—the unspeakable ego had to come from somewhere—but Izzy hadn't expected the haste with which she would slip from *technical enjoyment* to outright *gluttony*. She gave as good as she got, throwing aside the last of her self-control in the hormonal haze he generated, and giving herself fully to the experience.

Why not? Wasn't this a time for new beginnings? Maybe the new Izzy took more risks than just professionally.

Plus it had been a long time since she'd been kissed like this. Not just well but…fantastically. And with intent. What would it be like to channel all the competitive challenge between them into a sensual encounter?

'Oomph…'

It was only when she fell backwards onto her tiny bed that she realised something other than their lips had been moving.

'How do you sleep on this thing?' Harry gritted between kisses, settling himself awkwardly over her.

She gasped for air. 'Badly.'

Then it was all about the kissing again. And the promised groping. Pretty darned good groping, really. The kind of flesh massage that made an A-cup girl feel like a supermodel. She returned the favour, grinding herself into his hip until the heat billowing out from between put their clothes at risk of spontaneous combustion.

Harry sorted that. Within a minute they were both shirtless and the only danger was the threat of friction burns on flesh as they pressed hot and hard against each other.

And then, out of nowhere, he announced, 'This isn't working.'

Every minor rejection she'd ever had in her life congealed into an aching ball midway down her chest.

Of course he wasn't actually interested, she jeered at herself. *Why would he be?*

She reached for the edges of a blouse she no longer wore to pull them over her lace-covered breasts. But before she could do more than half shrivel at the finality of his tone, Harry pulled her to her feet, exchanged positions and then drew her back down with him.

On him.

She had no choice but to straddle his hips.

Oh...*right!*

Power surged through her as she stretched astride all that hard bare flesh, his eyes and hands roaming all over her torso, and then fell forward to pick up the kissing where they'd left off.

'You're very good at this,' she breathed as he sucked torturously on her ear lobe.

'Thank you,' he murmured against her neck.

Not quite *'ditto'* but infinitely better than *'practice makes perfect'* and so she'd take it.

The kissing went on for hours. Surely hours must have passed, possibly days. London might have sunk away into the Thames and been rebuilt on stilts while they were kissing.

'Iz, maybe we should slow it down a bit?'

His voice sounded pained and it occurred to her that maybe he was in physical discomfort. Certainly he had reason to be. She ground her pelvis against him in sympathy and whatever he'd been about to say next turned into an unintelligible gargle.

She'd done it to torture him, but all it did was add a burning kind of need to the pressure ache already resident between her own legs. As she repositioned herself more comfortably on him, she thought about her half handful of post-school partners, who'd ranged from eager but inexperienced to accomplished but in it for themselves. Yet, here she was closer to completion with a virtual stranger faster and more surely than any of them had ever inspired.

And in the next heartbeat, she decided how very much she

wanted to see if Harry Mitchell was everything he thought he was.

And the decision was liberating.

'We're not stopping,' she announced between heavy breaths.

Harry's eyes blazed hot and dark back up at her. 'Okay.'

Her hands reached behind her but paused at the snaps to one of Agent Provocateur's most artful and clever lingerie pieces. 'And you're spending the night.'

'Roger.'

Izzy took a breath, knowing what would happen to her slight cleavage the moment she removed the magic suspension. Knowing disappointment would probably stain Harry's hot gaze when he saw he'd been taken in by false advertising. But this was a one-night stand and he was getting laid and—PS— she didn't owe him anything. Least of all pendulous breasts.

She flicked the bra free. 'And you're going to show me whether you're worth all your own hype.'

The devil grinned back at her and, bless him, if he didn't keep his eyes fixed to hers even though a pair of boobs was now on offer. Secret points for that.

'Abso-frigging-lutely.'

Izzy pressed up on her knees slightly and then reached down between them, fussing at his belt.

'Look at that,' she purred. 'Something we finally agree on.'

CHAPTER THREE

IZZY STARED AT the broad, tan back just an inch from her nose and totally got why people would do the legendary walk of shame after a one-night stand. It was all well and good in the heat and hormones of the moment with a virtual stranger, but in the cold hard light of morning it was just plain…

Awkward.

Some time in the night she'd slipped from her exhausted slump across Harry's chest down between him and the wall. That made it impossible to get out of her small bed without clambering over him, naked and undignified, and tumbling off the other side. And the ornate foot of the tiny bed made sliding out feet-first just as problematic.

Entombed between plaster and hot male body.

Radiating male body. The longer she lay here, the more like a sauna her bed was feeling. Who needed central heating with Harry around?

She could wake him, but she wasn't at all comfortable about him seeing her body—especially her least favourite bits—in the full light of morning. Not that the tiny boxroom window let in much light at all but it was certainly brighter than the steamy dark they'd shared last night.

So then…what? Lie here, clenching her bladder until Prince Harry, there, deigned to wake?

Screw that.

Izzy arched off the bed and reached one hand beneath herself, grasping the edge of her pretty duvet—king-sized on account of her old bed—then she begged her abdominal muscles to cooperate and pushed up into a sitting position, dragging the covers up with her.

Cool morning air rushed in behind her.

Clambering over Harry's legs wasn't quite as confronting

as his hips and she twisted left—taking great care to keep the duvet between them—and half crawled, half rolled over his calves, her eyes firmly closed as she robbed him of covers.

She only opened them when the timber floor was beneath her feet and escape was in front of her.

'Elegant,' a sleep-thick voice rumbled from behind.

Busted.

'You sleep like the dead,' she muttered back over her shoulder, tugging on the pyjama bottoms that had tumbled to the floor from under her pillow with all the on-bed activity.

'I wasn't asleep. And you didn't even try to wake me.'

'I've been lying there, legs crossed, for eternity. You could have let on you were awake.'

It was clumsy but she managed to get her PJ top on, too, beneath the downy protection of her covers.

'And miss the Cirque du Soleil dismount?'

She had landed with quite a flourish. She threw back her duvet and only turned back when she felt certain it would have fluttered down onto Harry sufficient for everyone's modesty.

He tugged it back up around him for warmth. But the move looked too easy, as if he was settling in for a long stay. The rest of her squeezed up as tight as her bladder.

'Do you want first run at the bathroom?'

God, how polite was she?

'I went earlier,' he drawled, his accent more pronounced in the morning.

That would explain when and how she'd slid off him into the cool embrace of the wall.

'Bumped into duffel dude heading out before dawn. A friend of Poppy's brother. I gather she wasn't thrilled about him being here.'

So…this morning wasn't surreal enough. Now her boss was filling her in on her own flat's gossip. Her pulse started to panic.

'Hold that thought,' she said, holding up a hand.

The plethora of hanging things clattered against her door as she opened it and hurried into the bathroom.

Relief only took moments but Izzy hung out in there, standing on the toilet mat to stop her feet from chilling on the stone tile floor, gnawing on the inside of her cheek and desperately trying to pluck reality from this weird fantasy she'd found herself in.

What was the protocol here?

Should she ask him to leave? Should she ask him to stay? Should she invite him with her flatmates to breakfast later? All equally terrifying concepts. They'd had a fantastic night of what Tori would call 'monkey sex' and overall she was very pleased with her first crack at a one-night stand.

Possibly her last if this excruciating indecision was always waiting in the morning.

Why couldn't he have just tiptoed out like the coward he probably was?

Finger-combing her short hair and briefly checking her face for panda eyes, Izzy turned back for her bedroom and entered with the words already forming on her lips.

'So—'

But she needn't have bothered. Harry had re-donned his suit in the time she'd been hovering like a coward in the bathroom. He was just tucking his tie into his jacket pocket. As he did he pulled her ID card back out of it. And held it out.

'So, see you Monday?'

She just blinked.

'At the office?'

It hit her then. What he thought their single night had meant. How deluded he was. And how exceptionally arrogant.

She left his extended hand hanging. 'I'm not coming back, Harry.'

'Sure you are. We'll get on fine now.'

Was he joking? 'Now that we've broken the ice with the exchange of bodily fluids?'

Metaphorically. If not for the convenient condoms he'd produced.

He shrugged. 'We know each other a bit more now. Have each other's measure.'

Extremely intimate measure.

'Are you suggesting that our bout of horizontal yoga has somehow increased your level of professional respect for me?'

The outstanding quality of last night's activity really didn't deserve her dismissive words. But Harry Mitchell sure did.

He frowned. 'Izzy—'

'Miss Dean, to you, actually.'

Both his eyebrows shot up. 'We have four orgasms between us. I think we're a bit past Miss and Mister, don't you?'

'My *friends* call me Izzy.'

'And what do your lovers call you?'

No. She wasn't about to confess how little time she'd given to nurturing relationships with anyone. Let him think she did this all the time. Better than giving him any kind of hint that he might be special.

'They don't.'

'I'm not surprised if this is how you handle the morning after.'

Yeah. She wasn't dealing with this well at all. But the man was a boor when his mouth wasn't occupied with kissing and related pleasures.

'You know what? I think we should probably just call it a night.'

Or morning.

The dark brows sank back down again and then formed a deep frown. 'I don't understand what's happened here. I thought you were cool with something casual.'

'I'm not hoping for more!' she shouted far louder than the early hour would recommend. 'The fact that you think—in a million years—that sleeping with me was all that was required to fix the abysmal mess that is our workplace...'

Because that was exactly it. He believed *she* was the problem. He had no concept of his own flaws.

'We talked,' he said. 'We got along.'

'Hell freezes over infrequently. The chances of us getting along again are statistically smaller than before.'

Ah, numbers. The warm sanctuary of maths.

Harry slid the ID card back into his pocket. 'You're a strange one, Isadora Dean.'

She straightened until her spine almost cracked and curled her arms across her chest. 'At least now I'm free to be as normal or as strange as I care. And you won't need to trouble yourself with how I feel. Thanks for last night and all the best with your career.'

But he couldn't let it go so easily. He moved towards the door and stopped, a bare inch from her, and breathed his parting words down onto her.

'Just one correction, Izzy. I will always be troubled—intimately—by how you feel.'

'He did not!' Poppy's forkful of scrambled eggs suspended just before it reached her gaping mouth.

'I kid you not,' Izzy said. 'Those exact words.'

'Oh, my God. What a fantastic line.'

'Tori!'

'Sorry, sorry,' Tori placated. 'I mean, *bastard!*'

'Thank you.'

Around them, Ignite's busiest time burbled on, people nicking in for takeaway coffee before their Saturday jobs, others settling in for a breakfast as leisurely as Izzy and her friends. It made a confidential conversation more challenging but the buzzing noise of customers, clanking crockery and the music pumping out of the café speakers afforded some level of privacy.

Izzy hastily brought them up to speed with the events of the previous night.

'I have to say, Iz, given how thunderous your face was when I left the kitchen, this is not how I expected the rest of your evening to pan out.'

'You and me both, Poppy.'

'I can totally see it,' Tori announced. 'He was too cute. And that accent…sigh.'

'If I didn't know how clever you were, Toz, I'd be shaking my head now.'

'What?' She shrugged. 'I just appreciate pretty things. So, was he purely ornamental or was he any good?'

Insane heat flooded up from under Izzy's T-shirt.

'We'll take that as a yes.' Poppy grinned.

'I'm not comfortable talking about this.'

'You started it,' Poppy pointed out reasonably.

'I mean I'm not comfortable talking about the…details.'

'I'm sure Prince Harry isn't similarly constrained this morning.'

No. He wouldn't be. Something told her one-night stands came much more naturally to him.

'Look at it this way, Iz,' Tori started. 'Do you have feelings for him?'

'Not good ones,' she muttered.

'Did he treat you well when you were his employee?'

He'd treated her with the same under-informed judgement she'd battled all her youth. 'Not overly.'

'Did he ever donate a kidney to you?'

An eyebrow lift was better than an answer. Not that Tori was waiting for one.

'And do you ever plan on seeing him again?'

'Absolutely not.'

'Then you owe him nothing, least of all your confidence.'

And that was why Izzy had been Tori's friend since sixth form, when she'd first arrived at Trenton as a scholarship entry. Unassailable logic, no matter how disguised beneath the crazy hair.

'I guess not.'

'So spill!'

She glanced between her two best friends, opened her mouth for a mute heartbeat and then just let the words tumble. All about how good Harry had been. All about how feminine she'd felt when she was in his arms and how forbidden it all was. How she should have done the whole one-night-stand thing long before now, and how she would categorically not be doing it again. About how she was still secretly thrumming from his touch and more than a little sore in more than a few places.

About what a jerk he was.

The girls listened intently, exclaimed or squeezed her arm in the right places and generally fulfilled their obligations under the universal BFF contract.

'So Mitchell sucks in the office but rocks it in bed,' Tori summarised.

'Pretty much.'

'Well, context is everything,' Poppy rationalised. 'And clearly he comes into his own one-on-one.'

My wordy lordy, yes.

Until he spoke.

Ignite's maître d', Marco, swung by their table to check on their breakfasts and chatted for a few moments. But the impatience stamped clearly on their three faces soon sent him drifting professionally off to be charming to someone else.

'So...I saw a few half-hearted circles in the positions vacant section of yesterday's paper,' Poppy nudged. 'Anything interesting?'

'Plenty of jobs if I want to do the same thing I've been doing for years.'

'And you don't?'

Nope. Not even a little bit. 'Time for something new.'

'Out of finance?'

'I still love numbers but...not *in* finance, if you get my meaning.'

'I totally do,' Tori sighed. 'I'm the queen of in but not in.'

Izzy and Poppy exchanged a worried glance. But Tori would talk about Mark when she was ready. And the rapid way she kept the conversation galloping onwards said that she wasn't yet.

She sat up straighter, as if that would help the unwanted attention slide right off her, and spoke. 'What did you imagine yourself doing when you were a kid?'

Izzy didn't spend a whole lot of time thinking about her childhood. When she did it tended to bubble over with PTSD memories of her parents' water-saving *if-it's-yellow-let-it-mellow* flushing policy and other delightful poverty-busters. Clothes she felt sure were liberated from donation bins. Long walks to school and endless after-school jobs just to afford excursions and textbooks and some of the basics her school-mates enjoyed.

Isadora couldn't be poorer.

Playground chant, then, but it still echoed now when her origins came back to haunt her. Like last night. Her classmates pretty much had her pegged as the most likely to be pregnant by final year. *Like mother like daughter*, given the whole town seemed to know how few years there were between her and her mum, who'd had her at fifteen and then found herself un-skilled and unemployable at thirty. In fact, that was probably where they all thought she'd gone at the end of fifth form: to pop out a sprog.

Much more credible than a top academic scholarship to an exclusive girls' school.

Except, of course, getting pregnant required some boy to be vaguely interested in getting anywhere near her. And *that* required at least one who was prepared to look beyond the worn clothing and public benefits and work to fit in with her relentless after-school shifts.

And teenaged boys, on the whole, weren't much on work-ing for things.

'I remember wanting to do something with animals,' she ventured. What little private time she'd had as a kid she'd spent out in whatever field was in walking distance with whatever furry creature she could find.

Tori's jaw gaped. 'Please tell me we're not talking about cows and pigs.'

'Wildlife,' Izzy clarified, then, at their blank expressions, continued. 'You know, badger, deer, sparrows...'

Tori's memory cells lit up. 'You were always chasing down hedgehogs at Trenton.'

'And bloody otters,' Poppy added.

Good times. Hours down at the brook trying to find evidence of creatures in and around the waterway. Conveniently also giving her somewhere credible to go while her peers were rowing sculls or learning badminton or dressage or any other number of extra-curricular activities that weren't included in her scholarship.

Although... 'I'm not sure how many jobs there are where I'd get paid to spend my days crawling around under hedgerows searching for wildlife.'

'You could volunteer.'

'I was hoping to keep eating, Pops.'

'Well...maybe you could help some greenie group manage what little money they have,' Poppy improvised. 'Maximise it. I bet they're all great with animal skills but not so much with financial management.'

Huh...

That would certainly be different. But same enough to be not too overwhelmingly scary. 'What are the odds, though, of a group like that having a vacancy right now?'

Poppy gave her the look. 'Since when have you ever waited to be asked? Go work for them on commission. Fifteen per cent of whatever you generate for them. Until they see your worth and beg you to stay.'

'I guess I have signed off on enough of Broadmore Natále's sponsorships to know how the other side works.'

Tori snapped her fingers. 'That would have to be a professional advantage, right?'

'And no risk to them,' Poppy urged. 'No funding, no percentage.'

'And I'd have an in with whoever replaces me on the grants selection panel at Broadmores...'

Tori took a big swallow of her coffee. 'There you go.'

There was something terrifically appealing about being master of her own future. She was one hundred per cent *over* being told what to do and who to do it with.

Izzy lifted her chai latte and held it aloft. Poppy and Tori joined her. 'To the future,' she toasted.

All three designer mugs clanked together like medieval

tankards formalising the rightness of this moment. This decision.

'The future,' her friends said in unison.

He had no idea.

If he did, Harry knew Rifkin would be sweating blood that he'd shouted down the phone at the son of Broadmore Natále's chief and owner, Weston Broadmore. That he'd told the heir to the Broadmore global dynasty to work on his people skills.

Not feedback Harry had received with much grace, it must be said, but exactly the kind of honest critique he'd moved across the planet for.

Careful what you wish for.

Back home, the country knew him as Harrison Broadmore. It was only here in the UK that he was known as Mitchell. Not that it was completely confidential; way up the food chain at HR global they knew—they had to—but other than the head of London Security, who was sworn to secrecy, no one in the office knew.

And that was exactly how he wanted it.

His father was happy to humour him because he thought Harry was spying on international operations, and in Weston Broadmore's book that was a worthy undertaking. Harry hadn't bothered to mention that he was more interested in discovering whether he could succeed—or not—on his own merits. Without the illustrious Broadmore name backing him.

Without his father's money buying him advancement.

Or academic achievement.

Or friends.

Finding himself. Good old Dad would have laughed until his tar-soaked lungs gave out on that one. As if what Harry wanted mattered one bit. The company was his as soon as Weston Broadmore decided it would be. All Harry needed to do was turn up at the office, be seen, sign stuff throughout the day, then go home again. His father didn't much care what he did with his time in between.

It was all about appearances.

Just like relationships.

But the human resources director in London must have gone to the same school of personality as Weston Broadmore, because Rifkin was as tough and demanding as the CEO, he just didn't come with all the emotional baggage. So, while Harry was annoyed right now, he wasn't emotionally invested in that annoyance. It wasn't laden with agenda or residual childhood angst.

He'd stuffed up. This was the consequence.

As they said back home: *Fair bump, play on.*

Rifkin didn't sound all that surprised that he'd failed to bring Dean back into the fold—though his forehead would have creased like an accordion if Harry had confessed where his conversation with their recently departed financial whiz had ended up. Failing his mission came at a price: the bulk of Dean's key functions had been divvied up amongst the rest of Harry's best performers.

Rifkin had to know that the fastest way under his skin was to put more pressure on the people Harry valued most. That hurting *him* wouldn't be an effective tool.

So maybe Rifkin did know who raised him, after all.

End result… In the office on a Sunday, taking on a bunch of things himself to ease the burden on his most valuable workers.

Though, anyone watching would be forgiven for thinking that getting the jump on the week's workload looked suspiciously like staring absently out the window.

He crossed to his desk and reached under the pile of files for Dean's ID card and dragged his thumb across her pretty mug shot.

Nine days had passed since the party. Since he'd crossed a line he'd never imagined having in his rear-view mirror. Sure, Dean had not been an employee at that moment, but that was a mere technicality. He'd never—ever—become involved with someone from the office. Brief or otherwise.

On principle.

Something about pens and corporate ink his father had

hammered into him before he'd even hit university. Given his father was partial to dipping his pen wherever the hell he pleased, Harry always took that to be more of a 'how not to get caught' cautionary tale.

Then again, his father had no shortage of direct experience to reference. His mother had been a nineteen-year-old Broadmore intern when his greying father had met her and—if Weston's drunk stories to his high-rolling friends were to be believed—she got him wound up so tight he would have done anything to bed her. That eventual merger must have come with a whole swag of assurances—probably in writing—before she let him climb on top of her.

Rule of thumb for both his parents was simply 'don't get photographed.'

Two tiny pops issued from Harry's neck as he stretched it hard to the left. Bad enough knowing that about your parents without also having the visual embedded behind your eyeballs.

So...yeah. Not an employee; he was going to cling to that technicality like the life raft it was. Despite what the media suggested, he wasn't anything like his father. He'd never made a habit of sleeping with anyone for strategy and he wasn't about to start now.

Despite what Dean almost assuredly thought.

He couldn't even think of her as *Izzy*, because when he thought her name, he heard it in his head the way he'd been saying it that night. Half breath, half groan, pressed up against her ear as she'd made him come like a steam train. And reliving that whole experience sure as hell wasn't conducive to getting work done.

He tossed the ID back on his shambolic desk.

Isadora Dean was now in his past. He'd bear his punishment for failing to get her back with philosophical stoicism and he'd protect his team from HR's dubious game-playing by doing as much of the overflow as he could himself. He didn't earn this job without having some pretty decent financial skills of his own, after all.

Rubbing his rough face with both hands, he turned his

back on Canary Wharf and returned to the pile of files on his desk. Monthly reports, corporate partnership requests, financial statements needing sign-off, budget cash-flow analysis.

Some of it his, some of it Dean's.

All his now.

But that was okay. He'd work himself to death before giving Rifkin—or his father—the satisfaction of thinking him beat.

If nothing else came from all this he'd damn well prove what kind of a man he wasn't.

CHAPTER FOUR

IZZY SMOOTHED HER hair and skirt and took three deep breaths before emerging from the washroom on the nineteenth floor of Broadmore Natále's glass-and-chrome tower in London's Thameside financial district. Her old stamping ground.

Security down in the lobby had smiled extra broadly at supervising her sign-in and even the lifts seemed to whisper shut with an unnaturally enthusiastic swish. Welcoming her back. Not that she was going anywhere near her old floor down on twelve, just in case. She'd even gone to the trouble of calling Harry Mitchell's personal assistant and tried to make a fake appointment to find out whether he was in the building today, only to discover his diary had him out of the office all day.

Brilliant. Not a chance of seeing him, then.

'Tanya,' she murmured to the woman politely holding open the glass doors to Broadmore Natále's conference rooms as she approached. 'Good to see you again.'

'You too, Izzy.' Tanya smiled, polite but bemused. 'Best of luck.'

She'd grown accustomed over the past couple of weeks to the confused astonishment people failed to hide as she began appearing at the shortlist meetings amongst the big players, rattling the proverbial tin for The Lutra Trust, the little-known otters and wetland habitat preservation group she'd persuaded to take her on.

Otters? the conflicted little lines between their brows always seemed to whisper.

Seriously, otters?

She wasn't getting any closer to getting out of the boxroom, but she could at least lay her head on her cramped little pillow at night knowing she'd done a day's worth of really meaningful work. And after years of doing repetitive financial tasks that were as invisible as she'd felt, that was worth a lot.

Everything, really.

A different kind of reward.

'Thanks for coming, everyone,' Tanya started, in her amateur-theatre-on-the-weekends stage voice. 'Here's how things will run today...'

When the spiel wound up, the rep from the world's biggest human rights organisation was called in first. Izzy did the alphabetical maths and realised she'd either be ninth, as a 'T', or fifth as an 'L' depending on how Broadmore felt about definite articles. That meant she could relax for about ninety minutes.

Relax.

Deep in enemy territory?

She settled in behind the screen of a large pillar and muttered, 'I don't think so.'

It was nearly four hours before she was smoothing her skirt again and heel-clicking on the expensive floors into the conference room. She guessed she'd be facing Darcy McLennan from Communications and Kevin Busby from Marketing. They'd been a good team when she'd led them and she knew from experience that they were kind people whose only agenda was to make smart choices according to the departments they were there representing. Maybe she'd even meet her replacement from Finance, too, and it would be a panel full of friendly faces.

That took away some of her nerves as she pushed open the door and entered the room, her head high and a smile on her face. Darcy and Kevin both looked surprised as she entered, so she gave them an extra-warm smile as her eyes tracked from the right of the panel. But when she got to the left, she hit a pair of eyes that didn't look surprised at all.

Cobalt, piercing eyes.

Smug eyes.

Ugh.

Izzy stumbled just slightly but caught herself and continued on to stand beside the vacant chair on her side of the table. She greeted Kevin and Darcy with warm handshakes, then steeled herself and turned to reach to her left, her eyes steady.

'Mr Mitchell, how are you?'

Better the devil you know. Wasn't that what she'd thought all those agony-filled minutes ago?

That was before she'd realised she knew one of them in the biblical sense, but she'd soldiered on and delivered the presentation she'd practised on her flatmates until their ears bled.

Darcy and Kevin both looked mildly surprised.

Harry just looked bored.

'Otters.' He studied the glossy printout in front of him. 'Aren't they a kind of rodent? Feeding off the river bottom and skulking around in people's back-yard pools?'

'You just described half your social circle. You're still happy to do business with them.'

Darcy gasped but Harry's bark of laughter ricocheted off the fine panelled walls. 'Why don't you tell me what you really think, Ms Dean?'

Ah, sarcasm. She knew how to deal with that.

'Bottom line, the money The Lutra Trust needs to do great things on the ground would barely pay the stationery bill of anyone out in your foyer. Broadmore Natále would be a major sponsor with us instead of just one of a multitude with them. You'd never have to share logo space.'

Blah blah blah. She was clearly boring him.

'I'm going to be honest with you, Ms Dean—'

'That would be refreshing.'

He ignored that. 'You're not in our top five.'

The carefully schooled surprise on Kevin's and Darcy's faces suggested he hadn't yet polled them, which meant Lutra Trust weren't in *his* personal top five. Then again this wouldn't be the first time that he'd overruled his staff. It also meant she was screwed.

But she would be damned before she begged. 'Disappointing. But I'm just getting warmed up.'

'Really?' Only the slightest flick of his eyebrows gave her any clue that he'd not expected that. 'Not letting the moss grow, huh?'

'You'd be astonished what I can achieve when I'm motivated about my work.'

Tssss! Burned.

But he didn't even blink, damn him. 'I don't have to be astonished. I'm going to see it.'

'When?'

'When we cut you a cheque for fifty thousand pounds.'

Her respiration seized for shocked moments, but she had just enough left to stammer, 'I thought we weren't in your top five?'

'You're not. But you are sixth, fair and square. And, as you rightly point out, it doesn't cost a mountain extra to have you. I'll just shave ten grand off each of the others. They'll barely feel it.'

'I...um...thank you.'

'Don't thank me. You'll be working for it as our UK domestic focus. You'll cooperate with Darcy on possible media exposure and with Kevin on a style guide for all your visual material. We'll expect multiple public relations opportunities every year and invitations to any significant otter-based events.'

Wow. Had she been this much of an autocrat when approving previous recipients?

Her smile stretched. 'Of course.'

And just like that she found herself working for Harry Mitchell again.

Crap.

'Ms Dean, a word?'

Ugh...so close. She'd even called the lift already.

On a careful lungful of manners, Izzy turned. 'Mr Mitchell.'

He glanced around them to ensure they were alone. 'Nicely played.'

'What do you mean?'

'I mean exactly that. Well played.'

'It's not a game. The Lutra Trust has as much right as any other group to petition Broadmore Natále for support.'

'Is that why you didn't put your own name on the application? Because it's all so transparent?'

Heat threatened at the back of her neck. Only some of it was embarrassment at being caught out, because she *had* thought putting her own name on the application might have lessened the trust's chances, given how she'd left things with the company.

'The trust's EO signs off on all our pitch submissions. I wasn't trying to hide it.'

Much.

'I made it my business to check into the whole shortlist,' he said. 'Just to be sure.'

'Sure of what?'

'That they genuinely earned their spot. A couple of them have been in our top ten for years.'

'Because they're worthy and deliver a guaranteed return, not because anything dodgy was going on with their selection.' Too bad if she was defending the competition. She'd *chaired* that selection panel the past five years.

God, twenty seconds back in his company and he'd questioned her integrity and capabilities in close succession. 'Anyway, if it offended you so much why did you shortlist us?'

'Because you are a recently departed staff member with an axe to grind. Not shortlisting you could have been made to look like sour grapes.'

If she was that kind of a person, sure. And, naturally, he assumed she was.

'Then why did you grant the submission? You would have been quite within your rights—and within your policy—to draw your line at number five, as usual.'

The lift arrived empty and he herded her into it.

'I felt a certain amount of pressure.'

'Because I'm an ex-staff member?'

He smiled and then murmured between his teeth, 'Because we've slept together.'

It was only then she realised that he'd strategically positioned his tall self between her and the lift's surveillance camera. And that his casual palm-down lean on the little speaker/microphone above the emergency phone wasn't as casual as it appeared. He didn't want this conversation monitored.

If she didn't know him so well, she'd have guessed he was protecting her.

But Harry Mitchell only prioritised one person.

Offence surged through her body and fired her up. 'You think I would use that to my advantage?'

'I would.'

No doubt. 'I'm not you.'

'You used your inside knowledge to pitch your submission straight to our operational priorities.'

'I could have gleaned any of that information from your annual report. What you're suggesting is…'

'Is what?'

'Immoral.'

'What's moral about business?'

God, she'd found that cynical little snort quite sexy the night of her party. 'In your world, maybe nothing. But in my world I have this little thing called values.'

'Please. You're not trying to suggest you weren't hoping your professional relationships with your fellow panel members would have boosted you across the line.'

'The operative word there is "professional".' What she and he had done was personal. Extremely personal. 'Anyway, how could I possibly know you'd be on the panel? It wasn't in the appointment letter your office sent out.'

His eyes narrowed at the inconvenient truth of that.

'Why *were* you on the panel, Harry? You're normally the final approval before it goes to the board. Why are you doing your own grunt work?'

'Because my previous panel chair left the company rather suddenly and with no notice.' Criticism saturated his words.

'Your previous panel chair had nearly three months of accrued leave to serve out.' Leave pay that still hadn't come through since HR were dragging their feet on finalising her cessation. Probably thanks to him. 'But don't avoid the question.'

He shrugged, but his eyes didn't quite meet hers. 'If you want something done right…'

It could have been anger flooding in or the lift's sudden deceleration as it approached the ground floor that weakened Izzy's legs but, either way, she had to grip the ornate handrail behind her.

'Charming. I'm not even on your staff anymore and you're still finding ways of suggesting I'm incompetent.'

'I don't think you're incompetent in *all* areas.' The charm sleazed out of him.

But as her fury escalated something about his lack of direct gaze struck her. He was lying. So she pushed harder, right there.

'You're getting dangerously close to a statement I could use against you.'

'You wouldn't, not now you've got what you wanted.'

Again with the assumption that this was all strategy on her part. The lift doors began to open so she pressed the door's close button and kept her finger down hard. Blank eyes found hers.

'For the record, I approached Broadmore because I knew your system and your priorities and, yes, because I hoped that the people I'd worked with on the panel would help the trust get across the line. But not because I expected favours, simply because I knew Darcy and Kevin were open to new ideas and a persuasive, professional presentation. I had no idea you'd be on that panel and I certainly had no intention of using either my past employment or our brief…whatever…to boost my chances. In fact, I've been trying hard to put both behind me.'

'Maybe it's worth fifty grand to me to do the same.'

She stood taller. Past the ache his words caused.

'Maybe I no longer want your fifty grand,' she risked,

hoping like hell he didn't take her up on it. That wasn't toy money she was playing with. Fifty thousand pounds was future-changing for the trust. 'If it comes with the constant requirement to genuflect.'

'Ah, Dean,' he purred. 'Always such a team player.'

Was he kidding? 'Pot kettle black, Mitchell.'

'I'm sure the otter people wouldn't be thrilled to hear you're trying to return their funding.'

Okay, enough of this.

'Your reasons for shortlisting and approving our submission, paranoid as they are, are your own,' she said. 'I know why I came back to Broadmore—' though God knew that didn't look like such a sterling idea with benefit of hindsight '—and I know it was a good submission because I've been on two other shortlists already in just a few weeks. So I'll be able to sleep perfectly straight at night, thanks very much.'

'In that tiny, lonely bed.'

No question. He wanted her off kilter. He wanted her remembering how they'd flipped and turned and sweated together in that bed. And if he wanted it, she wasn't giving it to him.

'Eight straight, deep hours. When was the last time you achieved that, Harry?'

With that, she punched the door's open button and swept out of the lift ahead of him, resisting every urge to look into any of the building's mirrored foyer panels to see if he was still behind her.

'Looking forward to working with you, Izzy,' he called just as the street doors silently parted.

Yeah. Right.

CHAPTER FIVE

'OTTER FANCIERS ARE a dedicated bunch,' Harry murmured, casting a sideways look in the direction of the welly-boot brigade, criticism patent in his gaze.

Umbrage burbled up right below Izzy's skin. Sure, their volunteers were a motley bunch, and a little disorganised—and possibly only semi-effectual—but they were giving their time for free.

Her parents would have fitted right in if she'd found the courage to invite them. But calling because she needed something wasn't how she'd imagined getting back in touch with them after all this time. And this wasn't the first time she'd quietly put the phone down again.

Baby steps.

'Your staff are the only people here today who are getting paid to re-vegetate this waterway,' she reminded him with astonishing self-control considering what a jerk he continued to be whenever she was around.

Another two weeks apart had clearly done little to improve things between them.

'You don't think my people would be here if we weren't paying them to be?' Harry asked.

'Would you?'

He considered her silently before changing tack. 'You realise it was really only a few weeks ago that you would have been one of us, sloshing about with no idea what we're doing and fixating on knock-off time.'

Oh, she was very aware of that. And how much of a fraud she felt for pretending to be anything else, now. This was only her second re-vegetation trip. But it was amazing how fast her misspent childhood romping around the fields was coming back to her.

'It's a win-win. The Lutra Trust gets a helping hand on this stretch of wetlands and Broadmore Natále gets a good team-building activity.'

At least that was how she'd sold it to them last week when she'd first conceived the idea.

'A couple of pints at the pub is also good team-building,' he pointed out.

'But this is outdoors. In nature. On a beautiful day. And they're doing something worthwhile.'

'Everything they do at their desks is worthwhile.'

Maybe for their shareholders.

'Nothing they do at their desks will get Broadmore Natále's name in the paper, though.'

On the other side of the sodden bog they were clearing of weeds, a cadet journalist from the *Butterforth Crier* interviewed one of The Lutra Trust staff and one of Harry's team while a photographer grabbed pictures of the muckiest weed-clearing activity. Sure, it wasn't exactly a Sunday paper but it was a start. And he'd wanted grass-roots exposure.

'I thought you'd have put yourself forward for the interview,' Izzy commented.

His eyes instantly grew cagey. 'Not me. Better things to do than talk to the media.'

Was a village newspaper not worthy of his esteemed attention? 'Saving yourself for your *Time Magazine* Man of the Year cover story?'

His eyes narrowed and shifted, and not just because of all the natural light pouring down on them. 'Media is not my preferred thing.'

'Tsk tsk, Harry,' she purred. 'That's no way to get to the big leagues.'

His jaw tightened visibly. 'I feel certain that there are plenty of paths to the top that don't automatically involve public exposure.'

'You've surprised me, Harry. I would have pegged you for a man who loves to get his face in front of the cameras.'

In fact, she'd always thought him much more suited to a more public role than he had.

One brow lifted higher. 'Have you ever seen me do that?'

It didn't take much to get her *Izzometer* twitching. Something was off here. A man as arrogant and charming and… flashy…as Harry—even in that carelessly dishevelled Australian way he had—shouldn't have been shy of media. He should have been right out there in front, loving the exposure.

Hunting it. Playing up to it.

'No, I haven't. Why is that?' Unless he had something to hide?

'Media can be a circus.'

'Personal experience?' Because avoiding the media sure wasn't in any How To Get Ahead In Business manual she'd ever read.

'Direct observation,' he hedged.

'So any media leveraging you do off Broadmore Natále's sponsorship will be done by someone else?'

'Ideally.'

'Okay. Got it.' She pushed back a damp lock of hair and resettled her spade in the muck. 'Any other unwritten rules I need to keep in mind?'

'I'll let you know when I think of them.'

Before she could do more than open her mouth to quiz him further, the suck and squidge of gumboots sounded in the wetland behind them and Izzy turned towards a tense, interrupting voice.

'Izzy.' Alex rested one hand on his hoe and the other on her nape. 'What's next on the list?'

Which was, of course, man code for 'want me to hurt him for you?'.

Alex's perceptive eyes locked hard onto Harry. And stayed there. Izzy hurried to mitigate any growing tension with introductions. 'Harry Mitchell, Finance Manager at Broadmore Natále, our sponsor.' She leaned extra heavy on that last word. 'Alex Spencer, my…flatmate.'

He hadn't replaced Tori long enough for that to feel normal on the lips yet. In her head, Alex was still Poppy's hot brother.

'Another one?' Harry grunted. 'Just how big is that place of yours?'

'Small enough to hear clean through the walls,' Alex said evenly.

Oh, God...

She adored Alex, most days, even if he was far from perfect as flatmates—and even friends—went. But since an ex-soldier brought a heap more security to two women living alone on the fringes of Notting Hill, she'd made it her business not to complain when he moved in. Not about the toilet seat with obsessive orientation disorder, not about the stubble hairs that—like the sands of Afghanistan—seemed to get into everything in the bathroom she now shared with two people, and not about no longer being able to flit between the shower and her bedroom in her lacy smalls.

But, every now and again, having a protective best friend with an ex-military rottweiler at her disposal twenty-four-seven became just a bit too much to bear. Like right now.

'Alex had some free time today,' she rushed on for Harry's benefit, then turned back to him. 'Thanks again for coming to help.'

'I'm here on orders from HQ,' he said. 'I'd rather be sleeping.'

Harry's perceptive glance swung between the two of them, pausing for the barest moment on the gentle rest of Alex's hand on her shoulder. 'HQ?'

'My sister, Poppy.'

'Ah, yeah. Sisters.'

'You've got one?'

'I've got several.'

Izzy's head came up. That was the first vaguely personal titbit she'd ever had about Harry. If you didn't count knowing the size of his—

'Several?' Alex said. 'Jeez, I thought one was a handful.'

'Tell me about it.'

And just like that Alex's allegiance shifted slightly—just slightly—in the direction of the only other Y-chromosome in the conversation.

Harry held out his hand to Alex, who had to drop his off her neck to shake it.

That fact pleased Harry just a little too much.

'Looks like your sector is clear, Alex,' Izzy cut in before the two of them could launch into the full brothers-in-arms thing. And, astonishingly, given Alex had probably been up all night doing whatever—or whoever—it was that Alex did while the rest of the world slept, that was true. Clearly, his years in the military had made him super-efficient at manual tasks. Or he had a heap of manly angst to work out of his system.

Or maybe both.

'Give me another job,' Alex urged. 'Before I fall asleep.'

She consulted her list. 'We need an observation hide built.'

'A what?'

'Like a cubby house. But at ground level. For wildlife watching. Think you could manage a fast 'n' dirty little hide?'

'I excel at fast and dirty.' He looked directly at Harry. 'Sounds like a job for two.'

No! No, no, no...

No together time. No 'tell me about her childhood' moments. Not that Alex's knowledge went particularly far back. But he was more than capable of blurting out all her *nowhood* secrets, which was just as problematic.

How infrequent her male visitors were. How broke she was. How she'd floated around the flat all the next day after their one night together.

And the one after it.

'I'm sure Harry needs to stay with his team. This is a development day for them.'

Blue eyes twinkled. 'They're doing fine without me hawking over them. I'd be happy to get on the tools for a bit.'

Alex pushed upright. 'That sounds like a man who's built a thing or two.'

'Back home.'

'Australia,' Alex announced, wandering off with Harry in tow. 'Always wanted to go there...'

Let the bromance begin...

The only satisfaction Izzy got was from imagining the showdown between Poppy and Alex when she found out how abysmally he'd discharged this particular duty. Unless, of course, his real mission was to find out a heap more about their overnight guest. If that was the case he'd just positioned himself perfectly. That was the thing about interrogation. It often worked two ways.

Harry loped behind Alex along the edge of the wetland—resplendent in a pair of beat-up old Levi's, boots scuffing the sodden turf like some kind of outback cowboy—but he turned back long enough to toss her a troublemaker's grin.

The player is about to get played, methinks.

Lord knew what Harry would do with concentrated access to her life.

Ugh.

Mud splattered up and out as she slammed her pitchfork into a thick clump of watery weeds and she took particular delight in stabbing it deep into its core. The perfect tool for venting her suspicions about Harry's motives.

And though she had a lot to vent, there were, conveniently, tonnes of the stuff choking the little wetland. She twisted the fork to loosen the root mass, lifted it free of the water and plunged it down again, and again, deep into the weed clump's heart.

It wasn't Harry, but it would vicariously do.

Half an hour in Alex Spencer's company, and Harry already had a good idea of what Izzy's childhood must have been like and how it must have shaped her. Not that Alex was talking out of school; Harry practically heard the point at which the guy made the choice to spill. The clunk of decision. So, as casually as it was being delivered in between their measuring and sawing and hammering, something told Harry it was one hundred per cent deliberate. There was agenda in there somewhere.

'You really like Izzy,' Harry quizzed.

'Yeah,' Alex snorted. 'Because one sister clearly isn't enough.'

Sister. The message seemed clear but it was probably healthy to double-check. That hand on her nape had seemed über-casual but you could never tell with housemates. A living room was a very short and convenient space to cross.

'So, I don't need to apologise for anything?'

'About Izzy? No.'

Okay, treble-check, then. He pulled another batten across the joists and sent a couple of nails driving deep.

'For me, access to the friends was the upside of having older sisters,' he eventually said.

'Not that friend,' Alex swore, as solemn as an oath. 'Izzy's… different.'

Yeah, she was. Which made the casualness of what they'd done stand out in neon in the emerging observation hut. And which was probably the whole point of the conversation. But he wasn't about to apologise for what they'd shared, spontaneous or not.

He didn't do regrets.

'She's also an adult,' he said, carefully.

'Those girls have known each other since they weren't.' Alex glanced up, considered him. 'But, yeah. She is.'

And that was that. Protection implied. Threat tacitly received.

All obligations fulfilled.

'So, you knew her when she was younger?' he asked.

'She came home with my sister for a few holidays. I wasn't always around much but I met her a few times. Poppy's little shadow.'

Again, hard to imagine. When he'd imagined Izzy, he'd always pictured her in the centre of everything. Surrounded by people. Although, lately, there was mostly sweat in his imaginings. A lot of sweat.

And only one other 'people.'

'She's grown up, then.'

'With a vengeance.'

'Why didn't she go home to her own place on holidays?'

'That's something you'd have to ask her.'

And there it was. The big black line in the sand defining Alex's loyalty. He was happy to speak up *for* her, but not *about* her. That, more than anything he could have said, confirmed their relationship.

Sister/brother.

Something deep inside Harry cranked down half a notch.

'Not bad skills,' Alex commented, looking over Harry's deck work a short time later. 'You sure you work with numbers?'

'Courtesy of years of not being allowed to participate in sports after school. I channelled my energy in the workshop—'

Harry sucked his lips shut.

The truth had just slipped out, completely unguarded.

That never happened.

Alex lifted red-rimmed eyes. 'The school have something against contact sports? Or were your parents just overprotective?'

Just...

His parents were trying to protect something, right enough, but it sure wasn't *him*. He was the only boy after three sisters. The moment their mother had popped out a boy, his parents' sex life pretty much ceased. Clearly the concept of a 'spare' was outweighed by their long-standing animosity. And with a father as misogynistic as Weston Broadmore, his older sisters counted for little but corporate mergers.

So it was all down to him. Their future. His own. Everyone who worked for them.

And if something happened to him they'd have to start over.

And that wasn't going to happen.

So, no one wanted the heir to the Broadmore fortune breaking his neck in a rugby tackle gone sour. Or falling off a high board. Or driving in a vehicle less sturdy than the Hummer he was gifted at seventeen. The media deemed it a clichéd status symbol and judged him accordingly. In reality, it was the compromise he'd had to make to be allowed to drive himself around like a regular person. Either that or a Mack truck. And it was only his father's utter unfamiliarity with the kind of machinery that existed in expensive, modern boarding-school workshops that meant he was allowed to work with timber for leisure.

Or maybe Weston Broadmore just figured that a figure-head didn't need all his fingers to sign things.

'Yeah, overprotective.' He grunted.

Alex echoed it.

A good grunt between men was worth a dozen conversations.

And it was what finally made Harry realise why those earlier words had slipped so effortlessly from his lips. Spencer probably *wasn't* actually trained in military interrogation, it was just that he was as easy a conversationalist as Harry's own mates back home.

He glanced out to where Izzy and a fellow volunteer slogged away clearing a particularly weed-choked patch of waterway. He'd only seen her in full corporate mode or full party mode or, just the once, full naked-passion mode. But, she gave just as much of herself to this menial task as she did everything else.

'She always such a perfectionist?' he said without taking his eyes off her.

Alex's feigned obliviousness wasn't fooling anyone, and they both knew it. 'Yup.'

Yup. He couldn't help but smile; Alex was his kind of people.

'I think we're done here,' Harry said a while later, stretching the cricks out of his back and examining the finished floor of the little timber hide. Someone else would have to do the walls on another day but with him and Alex on the job it sure wouldn't sink into the bog.

'I should go check on my team,' he murmured. 'Thanks for the company.'

Alex stood and tossed his thick gloves into the box of borrowed tools. 'I might head home for some sleep.'

'It's middle of the afternoon.'

'I was up all night.'

'Doing what?'

Alex looked him straight in the eye. 'My best work.'

A laugh barked out of him, drawing Izzy's concerned gaze from across the brook.

Oh, yeah, definitely his kind of people.

'See you around, Alex.'

Or not, as the case would probably be. Loyalty to Izzy would almost certainly mean any offers for a pint would go unacknowledged.

Shame, really. Friends were thin on the ground, over here.

He glanced at his watch and then made a beeline for his team, half of whom were milling around, taskless, the other half of whom were still working like Trojans. No different here than in the office. Some people kept the air flowing, others just used it up. But, as he went, he made sure to pass by Izzy, who was pink with the afternoon sun and damp from good honest hard work.

That appealed to him on a level he barely understood.

'I'm going to let my people go,' he called across to her when she looked up and caught his eye. 'Thanks for the opportunity today.'

Thanks for getting me out of the office.

Thanks for getting a hammer back in my hand.

Thanks for your super-soldier flatmate and the moment of homesickness that came with him.

'Harry!'

He turned as she pushed her long, strong legs through the thick watery reeds. When she got to him she was breathless—still inexplicably pleasing—but it was hard to know whether it was exertion or nerves.

'Do you think you could see your way clear to approving the payout of my separation pay and leave?'

The anxious little gnaw at the corner of her mouth told him she wasn't comfortable having to ask for her basic rights. And the flip of his stomach told him he should never have trusted Rifkin's people to do the right thing. They were still smarting from Izzy's departure. Probably taking their sweet time intentionally.

'You should have had that weeks ago.' He tried not to sigh. 'I authorised it a few days after you left.'

'Well, clearly someone disagrees with that. I've had nothing.'

'That's bollocks.'

'I can assure you it's true.'

'I mean it's bollocks you've had to wait. It's your money.' He distributed the sawdust from the hide fairly liberally through his hair on his forked fingers. 'And it makes us look desperate.'

'Desperate?'

'To keep you. By holding out. As if you were going to change your mind and come back.'

His glance dropped to her lips before he realised what was happening. He ripped it away but not before she noticed.

'I'm not,' she bristled.

'I recognise that. HR is clearly just in denial. I'll get it sorted.'

'Thank you.'

He cleared his throat. 'No problem. Sorry you haven't had it yet.'

A month ago he would have added some kind of quip about how many lattes or pedicures she'd have to skip. But a month ago he hadn't seen this side to her. And something told him she'd be DIYing pedicures for a while.

Unless… He turned back.

'Are you okay for…? Do you need a—?' He reached for his wallet without even thinking.

'I'm fine,' she said, straightening up, her mouth tight. 'I don't need your charity. Just your action.'

Which he'd just promised to give. But she'd managed to make a well-intentioned gesture into an insult.

As usual.

'I'll see you Friday, then.'

That had her pausing and half turning back to him. 'Will you? Where?'

'I assumed you were going to the big Titan soirée? To make some new contacts?'

She blinked at him. 'Right. Yes, I'll see you there.'

And didn't she sound delighted about that?

CHAPTER SIX

THERE WAS A time that Izzy would have spent a week preparing for a party like this.

New dress. New hair. Facial, mani and pedi. Strategic hour or two in a solarium three days prior for that perfect golden glow by the weekend.

Not because she felt particular pressure to look good, and not because she got particular gratification from it. More because she loved the ritual. The anticipation. Party prep prolonged the fun. Especially with girlfriends along for the ride.

But not this one.

Not only was there no money to indulge a week of anticipatory expenditure, but she wasn't at the party to look good. In fact, looking too good at this kind of event could be detrimental to her purpose. Like an estate agent turning up to your house in a Ferrari. It made people wonder exactly where the money they were handing over would be going.

Parties like this one, hosted by the fund-sourcing group, Titan, were opportunities to impress but not parade. Make connections but not a splash. So it was important to look good…just not too good.

Her breath caught as her eyes filled with the sight of him, all suited up, striding through Titan's guests towards her. God, what was it about a man in an expensive suit…?

Her lids lowered marginally.

Hang on, that was a *particularly* expensive suit. Like the eleven-micron wool all over again.

'Izzy. You look nice.'

Any other party—any other man—and she'd have been offended. But with Harry it was totally possible that he was being simultaneously genuine and provocative. He just couldn't help himself.

'Hello, Harry.' The words were solid but her voice rose, breathless and curious.

His lips twisted. 'Is that a question or a statement?'

Ridiculous how her heart tripped over its own feet just at the sight of him. They'd only slept together once. Twice, technically, but only one night. And, yes, that night might have changed things between them—and her feelings about everything that had come before it, as new sunglasses changed the way you saw the whole world—but it was still a past-tense kind of thing. And yet there was the unmistakable thumpety-thump of her ridiculous heart. As far as it was concerned, the offences of their past were completely forgiven.

Extraordinary the difference it made knowing how someone looked when they came.

'No question. I just...that's a really nice suit.'

He glanced down. 'Are you going to want to touch me again?'

Heat rushed straight to her cheeks. 'No.'

'Shame.

'But you gave me such grief over the clothes hanging in my room, and that's...Brioni?'

Ka'ching!

'Every man should have one really good suit in his wardrobe,' he said. 'Isn't that what they say?'

'How do you possibly know that?'

'Sisters.' Those broad, Italian-tailored shoulders lifted briefly and it was all she could do not to fixate on how the skin over those nicely shaped muscles had flexed and stretched as they'd rolled around on her bed. Or how they'd felt under the curl of her fingers.

She tossed her short hair back and realised he'd started a new conversation while she'd been indulging her hormones. 'Sorry...what did you say?'

'Soonest begun soonest ended,' he repeated, glancing around them, assessing the room. Looking distinctly unimpressed to be there, actually.

'Not me,' she replied. 'I paid a fortune for my ticket tonight. I'm going to wring every drop of value from it.'

'Can I offer you a suggestion?'

The way he'd 'offered' her fifty grand? What strings would come with the benefit of his wisdom?

'Can I stop you?'

The lip-twist turned into a full-fledged smile that had her heart a-thumping again. It also brought his eyes squarely back to hers. The first time he'd really *seen* her this evening.

'Don't chase the money.'

'Meaning?'

'You want the best return on your ticket investment? Half this room is money, and the other half wants that money. You're going to struggle to get so much as a handshake here tonight. Maybe your hours are better spent networking with future clients?'

She turned and stared at the crowd.

'You're on, what, fifteen per cent commission?'

'Twenty.' Higher than most others in her field, but neither she nor The Lutra Trust knew that when they all agreed to it.

'Twenty per cent of fifty thousand will barely keep you in shoes. You need new clients.'

'Actually, hats are my drink of choice,' she quipped. 'But maybe I'll just get more funding for the client I have. Thought about that?'

'I have a better idea. Why don't you stick with me, tonight?'

The instant thrill the mere thought of that gave her was warning enough. It couldn't be a good idea. 'And what use is that?'

'Because this is a much faster way into conversations with organisations that are so busy scoping *me* out they don't realise they're being scoped in return. And this way, you're viewed as a conduit, not competition.'

That was true. Every person here was competing for the same corporate dollar.

'You're offering to be bait?'

God, she hated how good an idea that was. Not that she

hadn't done the maths, too, and come to much the same realisation, but she'd only planned on collecting cards and making
a few new acquaintances tonight on her own side of the guest
list. Chasing the money.

'And there's a lot to be said for the subliminal impact of
them reaching for *your* hand,' he went on. 'It redefines you
in their minds.'

She studied him again and any thoughts of him having
fallen into his role with charm or luck or connections evapo-
rated entirely. Harry Mitchell really knew his stuff.

'It's a good idea,' she acknowledged. 'And I'm irritated
that you thought of it.'

'Guarantee you it would have occurred to you halfway
through the night once you'd seen the feeding frenzy in practice. I just bought you a few extra hours.'

Her filthy mind didn't make it past *'I just bought you...'*

Imagine the things they could get up to if she was his for
the evening. To do with what he would. Desire coiled tight
right below her bellybutton.

'So how about it, Iz? Can you tolerate a couple of hours
in my company?'

Iz...

*Instant flashback to that word, hot and hard in her ear,
as he'd buried himself more deeply in her than she thought
she went.*

The entire evening, working the room with a man she'd
once had her legs wrapped around and trying hard the whole
time to pretend she hadn't. Knowing that brought with it a
funny kind of intimacy. A very personal connection. It was a
feeling she could hold close to her chest and savour for a bit.

On the inside.

On the outside she was going to fight it like hell. On survival grounds. Because while her stupidly optimistic body
seemed oblivious to the real world, Izzy knew enough about
people to know what a one-night stand meant.

It meant hands-off, going forwards.

'I imagine we'll be speaking with others most of that time, so…yes. I think I can manage.'

His laugh warmed her from her bellybutton inwards and he took her arm and slid it over the sexy fabric of his fine suit. She snuck in a quick extra feel.

Brioni… *Sigh.*

'Come on. Use me and abuse me.' They turned towards the throng of eager, bright smiles, but he bent long enough to murmur, entirely straight-faced, 'Especially the abuse part.'

Izzy snorted the champagne she'd only just taken from a passing waiter. 'Why doesn't that surprise me?'

Was it something to do with him being the most sexually exciting man she'd ever slept with? Or maybe, for those short hours they'd been together, because he'd made her feel like the most precious thing to walk the earth. She'd not even confessed this to Poppy and Tori, but, while the manner of their coming together was decidedly trashy and *un*-special, the way he'd made her feel in those moments was up there with the most memorable of her life.

Valued.

Worthy.

Equal.

Because he'd almost *seen* her in those moments. The real Izzy—with all her doubts and foibles and insecurities and lacklustre boobs.

And he'd wanted her anyway.

She pulled him to a halt just before they re-entered the thick of the crowd and turned up to him. The sharp line of his jaw under the designer goatee cried out to be touched. Even though she couldn't. Wouldn't.

'Thank you, Harry. This is really kind of you.'

His dark brows folded. 'No. It's good business of me, to make sure Broadmore remain the trust's exclusive sponsor.'

Right.

No secret connection. No mythical simmering between them. He was keeping his mind firmly on business.

Had she really expected Harry to be about anything other

than Broadmore's bottom line? Or was she just a little bit deluded?

She followed him into the throng and tried to keep her mind firmly on the task at hand.

But it wasn't easy with the words 'Harry' and 'bottom' swirling around together in her sad, smutty mind.

There was something disturbingly easy about circling a crowded room with Izzy on his arm. Not that he hadn't circled one hundred rooms just like it with one hundred women just like her—better than her, for the most part—but, before, those hundred women had always wanted a piece of him. There had always been an agenda and he'd always known he figured centrally in their plans.

Because he was a Broadmore, and even the good ones eventually realised what the money was going to bring them.

Izzy's only agenda was that she wanted the opportunity he was offering her this evening. And she was both open about and grateful for it. She'd more than held up her end of the deal in engaging the horde in her easy conversation, taking some of the pressure off him, and mining them to see who needed someone like her the most.

But she did more than that. All evening, she quietly helped the handshakers to put their best foot forward, prompting them with questions designed to highlight their strengths. Especially the ones who struggled the hardest; the ones totally unused to moving in these circles but doing it because it was what they needed to do to help their penguins or their heritage buildings or their trafficked children or oppressed nations. The over- or under-dressed ones with the sheen of terror dampening their foreheads. She prompted just the right discussion, asked just the right questions, steered them away from the inappropriate and generally facilitated the conversation.

She helped them shine.

For free.

And these weren't clients. No, Izzy was helping them out because she was gentle and compassionate and kind at heart.

And she didn't like to see anyone struggle. Even the competition.

She'd accused him of kindness, too. He was a lot of things he'd happily admit to but that had never featured high in his skills sheet. How kind was it to lie through your teeth to people who would eventually find out and feel foolish at best, betrayed at worst?

He glanced at Izzy's bright, open features and visualised them crumpled with confusion and hurt. Some tiny knife cut him inside.

Empathy, he'd have chalked it up to if he weren't sure he had none.

'It takes some getting used to, all that isolation. All that fruit and fish.'

The woman they were speaking to was still talking. Some island water-purification project stuck out in the Pacific or something. He forced himself to vaguely attend.

'But a few weeks back in the hustle and bustle of home and I know it's time to go back.'

Yeah, there it was. The shine of passion in her eyes. On the whole, people who were prepared to humble themselves like this to raise money for something or someone else were both ardent and dedicated. And he could live vicariously for days on their values.

Like a passion vampire.

He'd been passionate once.

They discussed her work for a few more moments until the woman perfectly picked up on Izzy's subtle but strategic straightening and excused herself and moved off into the crowd. Impression left. Harry knew she'd be hoping it was favourable.

Just a shame he'd barely been listening. He'd been too focused on the smell of the woman next to him and the feel of her soft body as it occasionally brushed against his. And lost in memories of their one time together.

Like the horny, hungry teen he'd once been.

'I hadn't expected to get an inferiority complex tonight,'

Izzy commented once they'd insinuated themselves in the service holding pattern around the busy bar. Back home he'd have been on the VIP list and drinks would have been coming to him on a tray. With phone numbers.

Here, he queued.

Small pleasures.

She frowned, hunting for the right words. 'They're such devoted, good people. It's hard not to feel inadequate.'

Really, that was what she got from tonight? Inadequacy? All he could feel was the usual sting of invisibility. Everyone here saw the chequebook but not the person holding it. If he ran a spot quiz as people left he felt fairly certain they'd all struggle to even say what colour his hair was, let alone his name. Not because they were bad people—clearly they weren't—but because there was something sickeningly… upstaging…about money. When it was in the room, people tended not to see anything else.

Not the charities. Not the media. Not the women.

Though any of them could probably tell him the shade of Izzy's lipstick. She seemed to have no problem connecting with them. Cutting through the seductive haze.

That's because she's not holding the sacks of gold, a little voice whispered.

'You're good with people,' he said. 'Don't think I didn't notice what you were doing tonight. Helping them out, feeding them leads.'

'Not everyone has the kind of experience needed to do well in this environment. They just need a bit of social facilitation.'

'Well, you're very good at it.'

She worked hard not to flush.

Wow. Had he really been so spare with compliments when he was her manager? His own body heat widened to absorb her under his skin. As if it recognised her gene code and wanted to reach out to it.

'I have good moments.' She turned brown eyes up to his. 'But everything they do is so meaningful. The most meaningful thing I did this week was hold my bus for an old lady on a walker.'

'You'd have made a good Girl Guide.'

She laughed. 'If my parents had believed in any kind of formalised institution.'

Here it was. The moment where he either asked about her family or he didn't. Or her school. Or her hobbies. Or her friends. It was how conversations were built. But the problem with conversations was that they were generally expected to be reciprocal. And not reciprocating was as rude as not asking in the first place.

But when the natural question after 'tell me about your family' was 'tell me about yours' and when there was nothing he could safely tell, rude was often the best option.

'That's the first time you've mentioned your parents.' He heard the words before he even knew they were poised on his lips.

So much for rude. Seemed his subconscious had other ideas. So the best he could do now was let the caginess commence.

She glared up at him, wide-eyed and sparkling. 'When was the right time, do you think? While I was pitching for funding or while we were having sex?'

Wow. Out-ruded on his own turf. That took some doing. So did intriguing him.

'Sore topic, I presume?'

'No.' Her response was way too fast.

'So I guess your enormous gratitude for this evening has worn off, then?'

Mental note to self: next time you're tempted to move countries so people will treat you like a normal person, remember how normal people get treated.

'I…no…I just—' This time, colour flooded her very English skin and backlit freckles he'd barely known were there. 'Okay, I'm sorry. That was probably overkill.'

He regarded her steadily and shrugged. 'Parents suck.'

And didn't he know it?

'They don't suck,' she defended, loyalty intense in those complex brown eyes. 'No.'

'But?'

'It's hard to explain. Thom and Christine are very unique people.'

Her frown was genuinely pained. And, inexplicably, that pained him. He held up a hand before she could continue. 'Full disclosure. I feel it's only fair to warn you that you have no chance of winning a game of "whose parents are the most dysfunctional".'

Stop. Dangerous ground, Broadmore...

Her dark golden hair tipped. 'None at all?'

'Zero.'

'Thanks for the warning.'

The speculation in her eyes screamed, but she simply turned and ordered herself a wine and him a beer—icy cold, just how he liked it—and made no attempts to continue the conversation.

He stared at the back of her pretty head as she collected their order and then stepped easily into the draught as he shepherded her with a hand at her back to a less crowded corner. Not touching, but itching to.

They sipped and crowd-watched and the whole time he waited for the inevitable.

So what makes your parents dysfunctional?

He waited.

And waited.

Izzy's wine was half empty before he finally broke the silence. 'Why do you call them by their first names?'

She stared at him for an age, and he wondered if she would answer at all.

'Their choice. They felt we could be equals that way. Friends. No societal labels.'

'But you didn't want friends,' he guessed.

That actually seemed to wound her. She glanced away.

'So what did you end up calling them when you were younger?'

The safer ground brought her gaze back to his. 'Honestly? I try to call them nothing at all. I've become quite accomplished at it.'

Yeah. He knew exactly what she meant. Some days when he was younger he'd have done anything to avoid using the words 'mum' or 'dad'. Just so he could forget for a few minutes longer that there was any binding relationship between them at all.

The older he got, the easier it became.

'I'm surprised they sent you to boarding school if they wouldn't even let you join the Girl Guides.'

Sure enough her eyes snapped up to his and he answered her unspoken question honestly. 'You met your flatmates there.'

Which was a careful—yet honest—way of not dumping Alex in it. If there was any hope at all of that pint he needed to tread carefully.

'They didn't send me. I went.'

'There's a difference?'

'A big one. But they didn't stop me when I won the scholarship. And for that I will always be grateful.'

As compared to…?

But the desperate edge to her slightly averted eyes told him loud and clear not to ask that. Time for a subject change, in fact.

'So I guess your parents are where you get your slightly herbal gene from, then.'

'My what?'

His eyes traced her body, criss-crossed in just enough snug, sheer fabric to be appropriately modest. Down at her left knee the fabric bunched and bloomed into a knotted flower. 'Teal and rust? Very earthy colours.'

He had to give her credit for not so much as glancing down to check her outfit.

Her eyes narrowed. 'First every man should have a suit

and now teal and rust? My gaydar would be doing laps right now if not for—'

If not for the fact he'd practically fused their bodies permanently together that night?

He lifted one shoulder. 'My sister Mags is a designer. Her place is a mess of half-assembled couture.' He reached out and traced the seam where the two colours met from her top rib to her opposite hip. 'I can even tell you your dress is cut on a bias.'

Brown eyes rounded, bigger and brighter than ever. But whether from astonishment at his ridiculous confession or surprise from his provocative tracing touch across her body he couldn't tell.

'Wow,' she breathed. 'File that under "things-taking-up-valuable-brain-space-that-could-be-used-for-something-else".'

'Tell me about it.' He chuckled.

'What are they like, your family?'

Clang.

Instant shutdown. Like a guillotine falling. He felt it and Izzy had a courtside seat, stumbling back unconsciously, gentle confusion glinting in those once shining eyes. But instead of coming over wounded, or gushing and apologetic, or instead of snooping further, Izzy just covered the moment with light humour.

Giving them both a graceful out.

As if she'd been apologising to others her whole life.

'Caught me. Trying to keep you talking so I can enjoy your accent.'

All his life he'd been a name first and a person second. Women, colleagues. Even some of his academic achievements were more about adding a Broadmore wing to his school than rewarding his own true efforts.

These few precious years in London were the only time he'd been normal. Just a guy. Albeit a guy who could have whatever he needed whenever he needed it.

He'd even had the crazy split-second thought that he could talk to Izzy about Mags, Carla and Katie without giving anything away. His heart pounded out the knowledge of how close he'd just come to letting part of the truth tumble off his tongue. How reckless he'd been with her. How that couldn't happen again.

Sleep with her, yes. Reveal himself to her, no.

That wasn't something he did.

With anyone.

He willingly took her lifebuoy. 'Some people find our accent harsh.'

'I find it incredibly sexy on the ear, actually.' Her eyes met his. 'And in it.'

He took a long swallow of beer, needing the gastric cold shower even if the alcohol was probably not conducive to keeping things wholesome. 'Maybe that's just the chemistry talking.'

She didn't shy away from the comment. 'Didn't we exorcise it all?'

'Not even close. We're a regular high-school physics lab, Izzy. Or do you just fall into bed with every Tom, Dick and Harry you meet?'

She kicked up her chin. 'Actually, you were my first Harry.'

An unfamiliar wave of unease rolled over him at the thought that there would ever be another Harry in her future. Or a Tom. Or a single, future Dick.

Wow, the stoutness of his ego apparently knew no bounds. There'd probably been half a dozen 'others' already. Isadora Dean was a sexy, intriguing woman. And the rest of the world wasn't as messed up and damaged as him, nor ruined for casual sex after his amazing night with her.

Maybe he should thank her.

It gave him more time to work.

He glanced back at the thronging crowd and saw a couple of furtive glances in his direction. And nothing to do with sex. If they stayed here they'd only stray into ever more dangerous territory, anyway. It was bad enough almost letting himself discuss his sisters without also going all verbal foreplay on her.

He'd broken a bunch of his own rules here tonight. Time to get back in the game.

He placed the half-empty drink on the nearest table and tossed his head towards the crowd.

'Come on, break's over.'

CHAPTER SEVEN

IZZY SWAPPED THE bottle of champagne she was carrying to her left hand and knocked on the plain, large door with her right. Nothing at all like the flashy Vauxhall foyer she'd entered through.

Lucky, or she'd have considered reporting Harry for skimming. No one working below the fourteenth floor at Broadmore Natále could afford a Thameside apartment like this. And Harry and all his team worked on the twelfth.

But upstairs was far less ostentatious than the rest of his complex.

The door opened with an almost surprised swish.

'Izzy? Hi.'

Breath puffed out of her.

She'd seen Harry in an Italian suit, she'd seen him in jeans and a shirt at the team-building day, and she'd seen him in nothing at all in the boxroom. But this was the first time she'd seen him as you would expect a man to be in his natural habitat. Casually dressed, his hair absent of the product that usually kept his natural curl under control, his usual goatee slightly longer than he'd normally wear it. Creeping higher up his jaw.

Same jeans as the team-building day, if she wasn't mistaken, but the work boots were absent, his long feet bare in the pale, plush carpet. But his black T-shirt was made of some kind of natural fibre so light it both draped and clung simultaneously. Clung to the curves of biceps and pectorals she knew from first-hand experience he boasted, and draped, below that, over the flat spread of his ribs and belly. Under the strong light of the elevator foyer the lightness of the fabric or the openness of the weave meant it was just slightly transparent, offering a hint of the tanned curves and shadow beneath.

How could a man be sexier clothed than naked? It defied logic, but here was the evidence standing right in front of her.

'Hello?'

God. Had she been standing here, drooling, for long?

'Harry! Hi.' *Outstanding start.* She pulled a few useful brain cells together. 'Thanks for authorising me to come up. Your security are quite scary.'

'They take their job pretty seriously.' Blue eyes fell on the bottle in her hand. 'What are we celebrating?'

'A gift, actually. For you.' Just to state the appallingly obvious. She took a long breath and released it on a silent groan.

'Come on in.' Harry stood back and she got her first glimpse of the apartment beyond.

Uh-oh. Back to impressive. Rich tones and minimalist, masculine furniture that took nothing away from what was beyond the enormous glass window.

'Wow. That's a pretty spectacular city view.'

'One of only two things I like about this building, really.'

'Why did you choose it if you don't like it?'

'Not my choice,' he said cryptically.

Picked by a woman, perhaps? Izzy faltered and glanced around again. No evidence of a female in residence. But behind all those closed doors, who knew? The thought Harry might have a girlfriend only reinforced the rashness of her decision to sleep with him all those weeks ago.

Just because a man *said* he was single…

'Pricey,' she hinted. But seriously, how did he afford it? Even on Broadmore Natále rates.

'I hate commuting. Buses particularly.'

'This is not exactly walking distance to Canary Wharf.' And that was not exactly an answer. 'Couldn't find anything you liked on the other side of town?'

'I have…family connections to this property. A good deal.'

'Handy with the tube at your back door, I guess.' The one she'd ridden here this evening.

'I rarely use it.'

She'd never seen him arrive for work—or leave—any way other than on foot. How, if he didn't take buses or the tube?

'Tell me you don't drive.'

'Not on the roads.'

She followed his glance far below them towards the pier. 'Truly? You take the ferry? Every day?'

'I have that at my doorstep and another one at work. I'd be crazy not to.'

'But that's commuting.'

'Not the way I do it. I'm not much on crowds, either.'

His words made no sense. Surely, he wasn't saying... 'You're kidding. Private ferry? Both ways?'

His dark brows dipped. 'Is this some kind of British cultural thing? Come to a man's house with alcohol and insult his home and transport choices in close succession?'

Oh, look, who was she to criticise his purchase choices? He didn't have sixteen different wool hats in *his* wardrobe.

'I just think you're missing so much of the London experience by not taking the tube,' she improvised. 'Or a bus. Or a cab. Like everyone else.'

Great. Now she sounded like an ad for Visit London.

His confusion deepened visibly between his brows. 'I'm not saying I've never ridden the underground. Just that I don't take it to work.'

His eyes grabbed the champagne she'd just been waving around as if it were a life-preserver. 'So, a gift, I believe you said?'

Lord... and all she'd done since walking in was poke at him.

'A thank you really,' she said, finally handing the bottle over. Critically conscious of how ridiculous that sounded after the past hundred and twenty seconds.

Why was she so nervous?

He looked at the label. 'Wow. Taittinger's. That's quite a thank you. What for?'

'For last Friday night. Four of those leads I picked up are now clients of some kind. I've got a full year of work ahead of me.'

'Nothing you couldn't have done on your own, I just expedited it.'

'Well…I'm still grateful. It was very generous of you.'

And he was still being generous, pretending that her mid-range champagne was remotely impressive. Taittinger's was the best she and Tori could find in Notting Hill's bottle shops on short notice.

He swung away from her and into the kitchen, where he plucked two flutes from a rack in his enormous freezer and gave the bottle twenty seconds in an express chiller. God, the fire station *so* needed one of those…

'It was completely selfish, actually. You made the whole night easier for me. I should be giving you the champagne.'

'I'm sure you wouldn't have struggled on your own.'

'I don't struggle when I swim either, doesn't mean it came naturally to me. I had to teach myself how to make the kind of small talk expected at big events.'

It was too good an opportunity to waste. To find out a bit more about the very closed book that was Harry Mitchell. She slipped up onto a seat at his bar. 'Do you go to many fancy events, then?'

It was only the slightest hitch in the level pour of bubbly liquid into the second glass that told her she'd made any impact at all.

'Benefits of a wide dating circle. Women I know always seem to be invited to one event or another. I cash in on the free food.'

Really? Maybe that was because he blew all his income on a fancy apartment and exorbitant transport.

'I'm surprised you didn't already have company on a Friday night, then,' she said, casually. 'If your dance card is so very full.'

Which only reminded her of how very empty hers was. If not for their hot 'n' heavy a few weeks back this would have been as close as she'd been to a man's bedroom in months. Not counting Alex.

'What makes you think I don't have company tonight?'

Her hands froze, midway to patting back her hair. 'Uh…
the way you poured a second glass?'

His lips twisted. 'You assume it's for you.'

Humiliation poured up her neck and she slid off the stool
immediately, onto the plush floor, her eyes searching down
the hall for the goddess that was probably about to appear.
Semi-naked.

'God, I'm so sorry…'

He intercepted her at the opening to the kitchen bar before
she could get more than a few steps towards the door, and his
strong grip slipped around her wrist then slid to half cover
her hand. She kept her focus strictly forward facing, hoping
her hair would have slipped forward enough to hide the colour almost certainly staining her face.

'Relax, Izzy. I'm kidding. The second glass is absolutely
for you.' He produced it from his other hand, icy and welcome.
'You were just sitting there being so wide-eyed Red Riding
Hood, I couldn't help a little wolf.'

She took it from him and crossed to re-examine the beautiful view, subtly pressing the frosted glass against the under-
sides of her wrists where the blood ran closest.

As if that could cool all of her in the little time she had
before—

'So four new clients, hey?' he said from just behind her.
'Does that mean Broadmore now has to share your efforts?'

She took two deep breaths before turning and lifting her
face to him. 'I don't think you'll notice. If anything it might
open opportunities for cooperative activity.'

'Broadmore isn't really a cooperative sort of firm,' he murmured.

True enough. They liked being up there with the biggest
and the best. Rarefied air. 'Perhaps it's a good opportunity to
learn how to play well with others?'

'Good luck with that,' he grunted just before his frosted
glass pressed against that full bottom lip, reminding her just
how plump and soft it was. Reminding her just how it had
felt on her skin.

That amazing mouth.

And not just because she'd got to enjoy it. Some men had nice mouths, some men had foul mouths, some men had talented mouths. Harry Mitchell had just the right balance of all three. Learned through experience, no doubt. Some pretty full-on experience judging by the way he'd coaxed her body to respond to him.

Like nothing else she'd ever known.

'Enjoying the champagne, Iz?' he murmured and she blinked back to the present. 'Your pupils have doubled in size.'

'Um…it's lovely.'

'And you were thinking about that night at the party.'

'No.' *Ugh, way too fervent.* 'I was…admiring the view.'

'London from above generally arouses you, does it? You wouldn't want to spend a lot of time on The Eye, then. Could get quite messy.'

'I'm not aroused.'

'You're standing here in my living room hot as hell. From just one sip of champagne.'

'Yeah,' she snorted, 'because I'm that easy.'

The tips of his white teeth peeked out of his cocky grin. 'Told you we had chemistry.'

'Hate to disappoint, but I'm not a slave to biology.'

'Then why are you panting?'

Outrage tossed her some much-needed focus. 'I'm not *panting*—'

'Please. Your breasts are heaving like some silent-movie heroine.'

Something about that word on those lips. It immediately reminded her exactly how well his mouth knew her breasts.

'Fine. Whatever. We have chemistry.'

His irises glittered as intense and vivid as the only tropical holiday she'd ever taken. With her first paid leave. 'Once wasn't enough, was it?'

'Once was plenty. We have a professional relationship now.' More was the pity.

'You don't think two people can have sex and remain professional?'

Ah...no! 'The two seem mutually exclusive.'

'Maybe you've just never done it successfully.'

Maybe she'd just never done it at all. But she'd heard plenty
of stories from friends about disastrous workplace flings. That
made her an expert once removed. 'Harry Mitchell, are you
admitting to serially sleeping with your staff?'

'You'd like that, wouldn't you, because it would lessen
the impact of this thing bubbling between you and I? Make
it less notable.'

Nope. Not going there.

'The only chemical reaction between you and I is the one
happening in this glass.' The words tumbled off her flustered
lips. Dangerous words, practically a dare, but better than them
doing what they wanted to be doing right now. What she could
see in Harry's eyes. What she could feel in her body.

'You think?' He stepped closer, closing the distance between them to just inches, and she tipped her head back to
keep her eyes on his predatory smile. He plucked the offend-
ing glass from her nerveless fingers and placed it with his
own on a side table. 'Your blood's not boiling with pheromones right now?'

'Actually, I think pheromones come from your skin...' she
whispered. But right now she'd nod and smile if someone told
her they came from outer space.

'Thanks for the biology lecture.' He smiled, close and dangerous. 'Shall we find out?'

'Um...'

Without waiting for permission, he lifted her wrist and
lowered his lips within millimetres of it, but he didn't touch
them there. He breathed in heavily—inhaling her—pausing
at the inside of her elbow, her shoulder, using her arm as a
tether, bringing them closer, his hazy blue eyes on hers the
whole time. His torso brushed up along her extended arm,
effectively bypassing her first layer of defence, and pressed
up against her body, warm and hard. His focus shifted to her

throat. It should have released her, being free of that captivating gaze, but, by then, the heat of Harry's breath had taken over sentry duty, holding her captive.

'I'm not convinced,' he murmured somewhere near her ear. 'Could just be your perfume.'

So he set about exploring other parts of her skin, nuzzling her neck, the pulse point under her jaw, nosing up beneath the silken sheath of her hair at her temple.

Liquid fire burned through her whole body but she resisted it, standing as still as her near-trembling legs would allow. His big hands branched through her hair, cupping her head, tilting it.

But still he didn't kiss her.

Tease.

'Must be pheromones,' he whispered. 'I can't think of anything else right now except you and that sofa.'

She spoke through the sensuous haze. 'There's a sofa here?'

His chuckle was pure gasoline on an open fire. 'A very comfortable one. Bigger than your single bed.'

'I'm not having sex with you,' she battled, but they were the most half-hearted words she'd ever uttered.

'No?' Cobalt found her, direct and hard. 'Mind if I do?'

With that, he swept her up into his arms and had her halfway to the sofa before she could suck in more than a breath. Then gravity took them both down onto it—rather abruptly—and that single breath came back out as a gasp.

'Sorry,' he pressed against her lips just before sealing them with his. 'Over eager.'

They were the kisses from the party again but better. Hotter. Heavier. Because they weren't first kisses between them anymore. Because they had each other's measure now. Because they had weeks of built-up tension behind them. All that chemistry he'd been banging on about swirled up and around them in a heavy, seductive eddy, stealing her breath and sapping her strength.

And because he'd admitted to being excited about it. It did

all kinds of squishy things inside her to hear him letting himself be vulnerable with her.

His mouth consumed. His hands owned. His tongue branded. The very weight of him on her was intoxicating.

Izzy writhed beneath him and it only made things hotter—harder—and her twisted dress crept further and further up her legs. His talented fingers were only too happy to help keep it moving.

But when he abandoned her lips to forage down her throat, her chest, over her fabric-covered belly, it roused her enough to curl her fists in his hair and tug him to a halt.

He lifted his gaze to her, and it burned live fire.

'You said no sex,' he slurred. 'I'm just improvising.'

She squeezed words out between gasps. 'I think that counts.'

'Semantics.'

And then he was gone again, busying himself with tucking her dress up around her hips, with shimmying free her underwear. She toed them down to dangle off one shoeless ankle, thinking vaguely about protesting. Thinking vaguely about twisting free, tumbling to the carpeted floor and hopping on one foot until she was far enough away from him to think more clearly.

But then that mouth got working again and she found herself incapable of thinking about anything other than how it felt to have him working so hard to pleasure her. About how the only other men she'd been with always stopped right about... now. How they assumed this was just a warm-up act.

And how unfair that always was.

But Harry didn't stop. He only got more focused. More intense. And her body mirrored his effort, cranking up and up as he worked so hard against her. Inside her.

'Oh, God...'

At least that was what she would have said if it hadn't come out such a gurgle. The cords of pleasure drew together, tighter and tighter, deep within her, responding to his touch and to the rasp of his goatee on her most sensitive skin. The novelty and sheer naughtiness of doing this right next to a glass wall, no matter how far above London, did their trick. Someone stargazing across the river on Millbank could be watching them through a telescope right now. It was even more risky and forbidden than their single liaison at her party.

Intoxicatingly forbidden.

Maybe she really had found her courage.

Harry resettled her thighs over his shoulders and her gurgle turned to whimpers, which turned to gasps and finally an agonistic groan as she couldn't stand another moment of his torment, no matter how proficient.

He rode her violent bucks and managed to keep his skull from being crushed between her seizing thighs.

Stroking hands eased her down off the brink.

Then he held her as she twitched.

And God love him if he didn't then slide back up the sofa next to her and collapse, just as satisfied as she was, against her neck.

No foreplay. No warm-up act. No not-so-subtle hints for reciprocation. His belt buckle remained totally inviolate.

Just…satisfaction.

She studied him from under leaded eyelids.

'I missed that last time,' he murmured, absently stroking the slight curve of her still-clothed breast with a finger.

They'd done just about everything else in their single night together. 'So you just thought you'd cross that off your list?'

'Opportunity presented itself.'

'What opportunity?'

'You. Here. With me.'

'And champagne?'

'And champagne.'

'So this was some kind of personal challenge?'

He pushed up onto one elbow and stared down at her. 'No. This was an apology.'

'For what?'

'For last time.'

'You're apologising for sleeping with me?'

That would hurt more if not for the fact he'd just been buried so deeply between her thighs.

'I'm apologising for rushing it last time. I can do better.'

That coaxed a little laugh out of her. Because it was ridiculously impossible. 'You think I keep score?'

'All women keep score. And they talk.'

'Oh, so you're worried for your reputation?'

Though, truth be told, she'd be blabbing to Poppy the moment she got home.

'No. I'm looking after you. I failed to do that last time.'

I'm looking after you.

Huh, first time she'd heard that in...um...ever.

'No, you didn't. You succeeded. Twice, actually.'

'More by accident than design. I was...not on my best form.'

She pushed up to meet him. More awake, now, as realisation struck. 'I think you're actually serious.'

'I'm very serious. I'm not usually that...'

She lifted a silent brow at him.

'Eager.'

There was that word again.

'You're truly embarrassed about your performance last time we were together?'

'I truly am.'

'And are you also on drugs?'

He brushed damp strands of his own hair from his face and smiled. 'Only endorphins.'

'You were—' *amazing,* but that was hardly dignified '—more than satisfactory last time.'

He dipped his head, just a hint. 'Last time was quite a lot about me. What I wanted.'

Of course it was. He was a man. And it was a one-night stand. She blew a few stray hairs from her damp face. 'Well, then, consider me very willing collateral damage.'

How surreal. Lying here with her skirt still hiked, talking about Harry Mitchell's sexual prowess *with* Harry Mitchell.

She twisted to look closer. 'Are you going all weird on me?'

'Just fulfilling an agreement I made with myself.'

'And what was that?'

'That if I had the opportunity to rectify things I would.'

And boy had he. 'And an apology card wouldn't have cut it?'

'Not even close.'

'Anything else you want to confess while we're talking?'

The blue in his eyes dulled off to a London grey and she missed the sparkle immediately. 'Nope.'

She swung her still-weak legs over the edge of the sofa and he helped her sit upright.

'So now that you've settled some inner score—'

His warm hand prevented her from rising, gentle on her shoulder. 'Don't get me wrong, Izzy. That's not the end of anything. Just the beginning.'

It took a lot to keep the rush of hope from showing in her flushed face. And it surprised her to even feel it.

'You're assuming rather a lot.'

'You didn't like it?'

Really, Harry? Writhing and gasping wasn't a clue?

'We've had sex three times now—' kind of '—but we haven't even been on a date. Or talked, particularly. I may not even like you.'

Pffff... But the lie gave her back some of the dignity she feared she just lost thrashing about on his sofa.

'We spent hours together the other night,' he pointed out.

'That was work.'

'You want me to buy you dinner?'

She shrugged off his hand and stood as steadily as she could. 'With a gracious offer like that, how could I refuse?'

He stopped her with a gentle hand. 'I get it, Iz. This is all backwards. Normally we *would* have had a more conventional date by now. And we haven't. It doesn't mean I don't want to.'

If sincerity didn't look like that, it bloody well should. Her lips tightened. 'You want to have dinner with me?'

'I want to get to know you. Go back a few paces. Like normal people.'

'You do remember where you just were three minutes ago?'

And what he'd said that first time.

I'm not looking for a relationship. A squirrelly kind of pleasure began spiralling out from deep in her chest. That he'd changed the rules for her.

For *her.*

'Yeah, Iz, I do.' He mussed up his already perfectly mussed-up hair with his fingers. 'Do you have time tonight?'

'For dinner?'

'You do eat?'

She quirked a brow at him. 'Try to. At least once a day.'

'Then how about it?'

Harry Mitchell was nothing like anyone she'd ever met. Arrogant and irritating and handsome and captivating and confusing, interspersed with moments of cryptic kindness.

Such a deadly, alluring combination.

'Yes. I have time tonight.'

'Great. Let me just grab my jacket.' He smiled. 'Do you like Thai?'

CHAPTER EIGHT

HARRY'S FORKFUL OF rice paused halfway to his mouth. 'I want to make a joke, but I'm worried you're serious.'

'I am,' Izzy said, polishing off the last of her spring rolls. 'My only aspirations as a kid were to get to adulthood.'

He blinked at her. 'What the hell happened to you?'

'You've never grown up in a housing estate, obviously,' she joked. 'They're pretty rough. At least ours was. But that's not what I meant. When I was a kid I didn't want to be a doctor or a scientist or a vet. I just wanted to be of age so that I could make my own money and my own decisions. Get a steady job, go to a busy office, buy clothes from a regular shop. Have a fridge full of food on the safe side of its use-by date.'

She'd started on her goal as soon as the law said she could get a job. Cleaning the kitchen at a greasy fast-food outlet. Her parents thought she'd been taken over by aliens with her burning desire to work. They'd grown so used to going without.

Yet she saw, every day, that *without* didn't apply to some families. And she wanted to be in those families. The ones who bought the burgers she scraped the hotplates for.

A deep frown marred Harry's pretty face.

Yeah. Poverty wasn't the most delicate après-dinner topic. 'Were there no good moments at all?'

'Of course. Heaps of them. I turned out okay, I think.'

His frown deepened.

'What?'

'I'm trying to work out what that angry edge is in your voice. You seem pretty accepting of your childhood.'

It wasn't anger. And it wasn't about her childhood. It was much, much more recent.

'It was what it was, Harry. I can't change it.'

Wow. Didn't that sound thoroughly Zen? He didn't know

it had taken her years to get to that happy place. Assuming this was happy. And if it was, shouldn't she feel...happier?

'Would you want to change it? If you could?'

'Our childhoods are what make us, don't you think? If I'd had everything handed to me on a platter I might have grown up lacking initiative.'

The frown wasn't shifting tonight, obviously. 'Is that what you think wealth automatically makes a person?'

'Well...not automatically, perhaps. But if you've never had to reach for something why would you bother stretching for anything? That has to change how a person forms. On the inside...' Her words faltered as she finally understood his expression. 'You disagree?'

'People with money still have plenty to reach for.'

'Like what?'

And with those two little words she got the distinct impression she'd disappointed him. But he masked it well.

'Happiness. Fulfilment. Love.'

'Important things,' she admitted. 'But luxuries compared to ensuring food on the table and heat in your house.'

'I'd consider love to be as basic a human need as food and warmth.'

The sincerity in his gaze pinned her against the wall behind her. 'Maybe. But you can live without love.'

Unlike food. Unlike shelter.

And she knew that to be fact.

His eyes didn't waver. 'Spoken like someone who had an abundance of love in her life.'

Instantly the old guilt rushed back in, heavy and uncomfortable. It was true. She'd been the centre of her parents' world.

If she hadn't, she wouldn't feel as much shame.

'Past tense.'

His handsome face folded. 'I'm sorry. Did you lose them?'

Silence ticked on as she stared at her crumpled napkin. Finally she raised her gaze and found no judgement at all in his. Just curiosity.

'They lost me, really.'

Yeah, he didn't understand. How could he? She barely understood it.

'I haven't been in touch as much as I'd like,' she tried to clarify.

'Why not?'

Such a simple question. Like picking up a phone and dialling it.

Simple.

Except when it wasn't.

'Our conversations are…' *Empty. Awful. Laden.* '…uncomfortable. They're so disappointed by my absence.' So hurt by it. 'And that just makes the next absence longer.'

Vicious cycle.

He stared at her, wordless, until she couldn't stand the thickness of it. She tossed back her hair. 'I'm giving you a run for your money on the dysfunctional parent stakes, huh?'

Indecision brawled in his gaze until he finally spoke.

'My school offered a residential programme for the boys of pastoral families from across the state and families from south-east Asia. They all flew in at the start of term and went home at the end.'

'How far did you fly?'

'My house was one suburb over. And I attended camps during much of the school holidays.'

Oh. 'No time at home at all?'

'A few days each holiday.'

'So, when did you see your family?' She hesitated to even ask.

'My sisters all went to the neighbouring girls' day school so we'd hunt each other out at lunch breaks and before they went home. Talk through the fence. My mother I mostly saw during holidays. My father would sometimes be home. Now and again one or other of them would come to school to see me.'

From all of one suburb away. Jeez…

'Wait. Your sisters got to go home in the evening and you didn't?'

'Dad thought it would be character forming. And he'd gone to boarding school his whole life.'

'How old were you when you started?'

'Primary school.'

'That must have been hard.' She knew it was. Because Poppy had been young, too, and she'd heard her stories of nights curled up under her bed weeping.

'We all got by.' He shrugged. 'It was a good school. And it had great security.'

That was a weird thing to focus on, surely? 'Clearly it made you very independent.' Enough to move across the world at the earliest opportunity.

'I'm sure that was the point. I suspect my father feared I'd be raised as one of the girls if I stayed at home.'

'How many sisters did you say you had?'

His eyes shifted left briefly. 'I didn't. A few.'

She gave him her best Tori look. 'So many you can't remember, exactly?'

'What difference does it make?'

'It doesn't make a *difference*, Harry. It makes a *conversation*.' But she wasn't going to force him to unwrap the mystery parcel that was Harry Mitchell. He'd start peeling when he was ready.

A pretty waitress came and cleared their empty entrée dishes away on a shy smile. Izzy couldn't help herself. She stacked them and moved the cutlery to the top. The woman bowed and thanked her in a small voice.

'Listen, Harry, I'm sorry if I offended you. I was speaking generally about people with money.'

The tension didn't dissipate any. 'Why would I be offended?'

'Expensive boarding school. Absent parents. Flitting off to London to work. I'm guessing you weren't raised by delicatessen owners.'

His careful smile belied the tension in the rest of his face. 'It's Australia, Iz. Land of hard work and opportunity. A delicatessen owner is likely to be just as rich as a real-estate mogul.'

She took a breath. 'Is that what your father was? A mogul?'

Something indefinable blazed in his eyes. Some desire she couldn't quite put her finger on. But he glanced at the waitress, who refreshed their drinks and when they returned to hers they were empty again.

'You seem very interested in my net worth,' he said easily. 'First you grill me back in the apartment, now this. What's with that?'

Grill? 'I'm not—'

'And for someone who apparently doesn't have a lot of time for the wealthy you've sure gone out of your way to emulate them.'

She pressed her lips shut.

'The flash clothes, the steady diet of champagne, the up-market address…'

'Our *upmarket* address has free-ranging rodents and I sleep in a boxroom,' she reminded him.

'Only very recently. A turret, I believe you said, previously?'

Her parents' faces returned, large and critical, in her mind. The same unvoiced criticism alive in their faces. She shoved them away. 'Poppy and Alex had to lose someone they loved for that flat, so it came at quite a price. Besides, is it wrong to enjoy nice things if I can afford them?'

And sell them online when she couldn't.

'Not at all. But I think you're going to need to pick either side of the fence on the question of the comparative merits of wealth and stick to it.'

She let her eyebrows do the talking. 'Are you suggesting I'm a hypocrite?'

'I'm suggesting that for someone who is so okay with her upbringing and so down on wealth you've spent a lot of time creating the trappings of it around you.'

Embarrassment flushed through her. Because of how right he was. 'Says the man with the Thameside apartment.'

'Hey, I've worked just as hard as you studying and build-ing my career. The difference is I don't judge you by what you do or don't have.'

'You're judging me now,' she challenged. 'And finding me lacking.'

And wasn't that just a little bit too familiar?

'It's not judgement, Iz. I'm just getting to know you.'

'With a bit of casual character assassination?'

He studied her closely. 'I'm sorry. I just wanted to make the point that acceptance and tolerance go both ways. Judg-ing people by their actions not their means.'

That was what she'd been expecting of others her whole life. How could she reasonably do less?

She took a deep, long breath. 'Look...I know I went a little bit crazy there for a while with all the spending. Everything I know about having money I learned on television. I figured that all those people telling me it wouldn't make me happy just wanted to keep more of it for themselves. I know every-one has their demons and challenges...'

Deep down somewhere, she really did know that.

Her earnest expression seemed to work a kind of magic on him and his whole body relaxed. 'Hard to resist buying up all the things you never had, I guess.'

'They were a great couple of years.'

His chuckle tickled somewhere left of her sternum. 'And now?'

'Now I'm starting to see the value in what I *do*, not what I earn.'

Not too dissimilar to what her father tried to instil in her. Except he was talking about the kind of person you were, not what you did for a living. Because...well, because he didn't have a living.

An accident driving his lorry and the nine pins in his spine had sorted that for ever.

His focus grew even more intent. 'And that's important to you?'

'Self-respect for the job you do every day is just as important as self-respect for the life you lead. Or the choices you make. Or the people you make relationships with.'

He nodded, as if it made perfect sense, but then pointed out, 'Self-respect won't get you the turret back.'

She sighed. 'The turret is occupied now, anyway.'

'Really?'

'Isaac. The friend of Alex's you met. Temporary, while his own place is being painted.'

A man. In *her* room. Dropping his man fluff all over her carpet.

'You could come back to Broadmore in a heartbeat, you know that, right? We'd find you a different role. A different section. Something you could enjoy. And with a raise.'

She twisted around to face him more directly. 'Leaving the firm was more about *me* than the job, Harry.' Despite what she'd written on his window. 'You can't do much about fixing that.'

Except that—somehow—just being with him had started to feel a lot like fixing. Those loose, lost threads she carried around permanently inside were beginning to twist into a stronger, surer twine.

He refilled her glass from the pitcher. 'Here's to your four new clients, then. And the independence they represent.'

She held hers aloft. 'And to self-respect.'

He held her eyes as his beer clanked against her glass. 'To self-respect.'

Self-respect.

Yeah, he knew all about that. Or the desire for it, anyway. Wasn't that what being in London was all about? Earning his future instead of having it handed to him on a gilt platter? Getting inside the company he would one day be expected to lead. Getting to know the people and problems there.

The Vauxhall apartment was the price he'd paid to get here. As much a deal-breaker as the Hummer. The Broadmore heir needed a reasonable level of security and the flash apartment was a good way of ensuring he didn't end up in a share house with felons. Harry was reasonably certain that someone else on his floor was Broadmore security personnel. He had no names, just that occasional skin-tingle that said he was being watched.

It galled that he wasn't free to explain any of that to Izzy. She'd have to go on what was only partly true.

A private water taxi east to Canary Wharf and back again every day did cost money; money a normal person wouldn't waste. But, for him, the time it took to ride two underground lines all the way to work and back again or to take the chugging, endlessly stopping ferries...that was a waste. Of his time. Inefficient.

And he was all about efficiency.

Or was he just deluding himself? Was it just part of the same contempt he felt for the cash that filled his plate and padded out the place in his childhood where love should have been? It was meaningless, expendable.

Literally.

Money was the reason women flocked to him back home. Money was the reason clients flocked to him now.

It was the thing that gave him value.

Wasn't it?

Coming to London had tested that. Without his name and his father's bankrolling behind him, he'd managed to blend in a treat with everyone else in the office. Turned out he was quite unexceptional without his money. Not bad, but nothing outstanding. Solid but not remarkable at work, good but not breathtaking at play. The women who had once flapped around Harrison Broadmore like moths were pretty much AWOL in Harry Mitchell's world. The professional fawning he'd once enjoyed also mysteriously absent.

And he knew that because he tested it regularly. To see if it had ever been *him*, at all. To some people, that came off as arrogant. But really he just wanted to see what happened when he pushed people who weren't paid to keep smiling.

Or kissed someone who wasn't reaching for his wallet.

'Harry?'

He snapped back to the present.

'I was wondering why we are eating here rather than in the fancy restaurant in your building.'

'The view may be fancy but the food is much better here. Would you rather we were there?'

'No. I can get the view for free in your apartment.'

Ha. 'That's not the comment of a spendthrift.'

'Well, there's spending...' she smiled '...and there's wasting.'

'And a revolving restaurant would be a waste?'

'If it's not as good as this *kway teow*, yeah.'

'I love that you are happy to tuck in in front of me.'

'Well...my morning run just doubled but I'm not going to walk away from a good meal opportunity.'

'That's not something I hear from most women.'

Two tiny lines crossed like her chopsticks between her brows.

Nice one, moron. Remind her how many women you've taken to dinner.

Or just taken.

She gathered more noodles into a pile. 'Christine promised me I'd have curves when I grew up. So did the school nurse. And all my friends.'

'Are we talking about breasts?'

'Breasts. Hips, the curve of a nice bum. I endured being scrawny all my childhood, and a lovely shape as an adult was supposed to be the pay-off.'

'I wouldn't call you scrawny.'

Not by model standards. And he'd know.

'Are you about to say "gamine"?'

'No. That sounds like something that should be on the menu. I was going to say "slender".'

'Because you're from the sixties?'

'Lean?'

'Like this beef?'

'You're killing me. How about "willowy"?'

Her long neck elongated just slightly as she tipped her head and tested the word on her tongue. 'I could live with that.'

'Another thing some people would kill for. Your body.'

He sure would. Strong and resilient and healthy. And that thought just made him want to test how many ways it bent.

He cleared his throat.

'That's because "people" don't know what it's like to have to have everything you wear altered to make up for being shaped like a ruler.'

'I'm sure I managed to find hips to hang on to that night in your flat.'

Gorgeous heat flamed up her jaw. 'Shh! Do you mind? We're not alone in this restaurant.'

Just talking dirty to Izzy was a turn-on. He didn't even need to touch her and his body would start to get involved. 'More's the pity.'

'Anyway. I wasn't fishing for compliments, thanks very much. So you can save your breath. And I can see you're finished but I'm not so you'll just have to sit tight.'

'Go for it. I'll just watch.'

He steepled his fingers below his chin and rested it there, giving her his most infuriating smile.

'That's just rude.'

He was getting to her? Good. Revenge was sweet. 'It's polite. I don't want to rush you.'

She ignored him completely for the next mouthful of flat noodles and vegetable. But by the one after that she'd become aware of the intense focus he was placing on her slightly Thai-greased lips, the extra smile he gave her when she tried to lick it demurely off.

She pressed a napkin to her mouth instead, robbing him of his fun. 'Okay, I think I'm done.' The napkin hit the table with a silent thud.

'Finish your meal, Izzy.'

'No. You're making it uncomfortable.'

'Why? Because I'm watching you?'

'It's the way you're watching.'

'You don't like the attention?'

'It's…predatory.'

'You say that like it's a bad thing. Am I the only one who remembers what happened before dinner?'

She glanced around them, furious colour staining her skin. 'No.'

'Am I the only one anticipating what's going to happen after dinner?'

'Nothing's going to happen while I have a belly full of Thai food. Bad planning on your part.'

'Ah, but the night is long.'

'Sadly, the walk back to your place is not.'

'We can take the scenic route.'

'Really? There's something more scenic than the shabby lane you brought me up to this restaurant?'

'Want to find out?'

It took only minutes to settle up, walk back towards the Albert Embankment and turn towards Lambeth Bridge in the distance. Away from his apartment.

'I walk the bridges a couple of times a week,' he told her. 'When I can't sleep.'

She peered up at him sideways. 'And how often can't you sleep?'

More than he cared to admit. 'Often enough.'

'Christine's the same. She can't sleep in the city.'

'So she doesn't visit?' Educated guess.

Discomfort swamped Izzy's face, even under the odd glow of the embankment lights. 'Too much white noise or…something.'

Back home if he was having trouble sleeping he'd pick up the phone and within twenty minutes he had nature's sedative knocking on his door. But women weren't as eager to get out of bed for a midnight booty call with middle management Harry Mitchell. Consequently, he spent a lot of time staring at the roof of his apartment. Or walking between Lambeth and Vauxhall bridges.

Maybe he'd always been a bad sleeper but was just too spent to notice?

Admiring the floodlit, art deco design of the nearest building ate up valuable minutes of conversation until they got clear of it. Then a noise up a side street startled them both and Izzy's healthy pace stuttered.

'Are we safe walking here?'

'Are you kidding? MI6 headquarters on one side of the Thames and MI5 on the other. Between the lighting and surveillance, these embankments are about as bright and secure as any in London. Plus you have me for protection.'

He probably should have been offended at her insta-laugh.

'I guess you *could* always throw spreadsheets at them. And tie them up with your unassailable logic.'

God, her sarcasm was a turn-on. Every part of him was tingling. But he wasn't going to let her off that easy. 'Or I could take them down with my martial arts training.'

She pulled him to a halt. 'Really?'

And here they were again. The moment where he could tell her the truth. He'd already blurted more than he'd planned back at the restaurant, but she'd so bravely unloaded the skeleton from her closet it seemed impossible not to reciprocate a little.

Maybe that was the trick. Just little pieces. Meaningless unless you put the puzzle together. Which he'd never let her do.

'Jiu-jitsu. Black belt.'

'*Black* belt?'

'Relax,' he said as they started moving again. 'Lots of people have them these days. It's not a big deal.'

Except that it was the one physical outlet that his father deemed the benefits to outweigh the risks. Thank God or he would have had to resort to music or drama to fill those long empty hours each evening. And a Shakespearean soliloquy would have been no use whatsoever for impressing Izzy. And he liked nothing better than her brown eyes widening with surprise.

Unless it was them widening with lust.

'But it's not a small deal,' she said. 'That takes masses of discipline.'

'You think I lack discipline?'

Yep. Clearly she did.

'Can you show me some moves?'

He glanced around. 'Someone's going to report me for threatening you.'

She hoisted herself up on the stone embankment barrier and crossed her long legs. 'When I look this relaxed?'

'Nuh-uh.' He lifted her down and she slid the length of his body. Nice bonus. 'If I do this, you do it with me.'

He turned to face her, bowed briefly, and then locked eyes with her.

Her pretty brow lowered. 'What am I doing?'

'Come at me with menace.'

'Then *I'll* get reported.'

'Come on, nothing half-hearted. Like you mean it.'

Izzy glanced around and then back to him uncertainly. But as she opened her mouth to protest she shot forward with as much menace as a daisy and went to shoulder him off balance. But he'd been doing this a long time. The second she made body contact he curled into it, twisted around behind her and locked one arm across her chest and the other around her waist, and his leg took hers out from under them.

They went down like a tangled, gentle mess, his body wearing most of the impact.

'Is this your idea of foreplay?' she gritted from the green grass.

'You wanted a demo.'

'Were you so eager to get me on my back?'

'Just saving time.' He grinned.

Steady eyes regarded him. 'You're very confident that I'll be sleeping with you tonight.'

'You're still with me, aren't you?'

'I have eighty kilos of unexpected ego on top of me.'

'I've been very open with my intentions. If you weren't on

board with the idea of us having sex again you'd have found a polite way to extricate yourself before the noodles.'

'Well, it's not happening here, so how about letting me up?'

He rolled to one side and pulled her with him to his feet. 'Next time you'll know better than to question a man's martial arts prowess.'

'I'm duly impressed. I guess I should be grateful you only bruised me.'

He was back by her side in a heartbeat. 'I hurt you?'

Damn. He'd lowered her as gently as he could.

His concern seemed to confuse her, more than anything. 'No. Just my pride.'

'Come on.'

It was the most natural thing on the planet to take Izzy's hand then, and then keep it even once he'd pulled her to her feet. He couldn't remember the last time he'd held someone's hand. It felt…

Normal.

Like two regular people walking and talking.

They stayed like that all the way to Lambeth Bridge, fingers entwined, arms brushing.

It was amazing what you could say while saying nothing of consequence. Every cell in his body wanted to answer her questions as Harrison, not Harry. Wanted to trust her with his truth. But he'd worked hard to create his London life, for as long as he'd be able to keep it, and he shouldn't be having thoughts of just throwing it away lightly.

Besides…he'd warned her he didn't do relationships and he meant it. Whatever this was would probably flare out in a week. So what was the point?

Inexplicable sadness washed through him like the waters below the bridge.

'Want to walk to the wheel?'

She turned away and moved towards the opposite bank from the giant wheel lit up like a Christmas tree. 'The London Eye gets quite enough attention without me adding to its ego.'

'I bet you think that about me.'

'And I stand by that.'

She didn't give him an inch. All the way back up Millbank. It was a kind of playful repartee he'd not had since hanging out with his sisters before the great separation into different schools. There was no gushing, no overt innuendo, the only touching was where their hands met and their arms brushed. She made him work, every step of the conversation.

He'd almost forgotten how.

It was sexy as hell. And his mouth was practically dry from all the talking.

One sure way to fix that.

'Hold up.'

He pulled her to a halt in front of the art gallery and walked her, backwards, into the giant stone plinth on the left of the stairs. A flood light on the plinth top blazed a bright glow onto the white stone building, casting a convenient shadow immediately below it. But not so much that Izzy wasn't bathed in an ethereal reflected glow.

'Are you going to kiss me?' she breathed.

His eyes flicked over every part of her that wasn't pressed by his body to the stone. 'Sure am.'

'Anytime soon?'

It took no effort at all to fulfil her request. She even met him halfway before settling back against the stone and letting him press forward into her. Her mouth was like fire: scorching and dangerous. Still with a hint of Thai chilli. And more than a little bit addictive. It wasn't the mouth of a practised expert—and for that he was grateful—but Izzy was no novice, either. She was like Goldilocks. Just right. She kissed as she laughed—honest and without agenda.

But really, really well.

Hence his official Izzy addiction.

Her hands snaked up to link around his neck, crushing their chests together, her hard nipples celebrating their closeness. In case there was any doubt she was into him.

Someone walked past behind them and chuckled; he didn't care. All he knew were Izzy's lips. The feel of her body against his. The burn of need coiling outwards from low in his gut. Not *want*, which he was plenty accustomed to.

Need.

This was a woman he could fall for. Hard.

If he was the kind of guy who could afford to fall hard.

Izzy stimulated him intellectually, aroused him physically and offered him what he'd never had much of in his life. Honesty. Integrity.

Her loyalty, if he let her.

And it didn't hurt that she thought he was pretty good in bed. She didn't waste time with the whole *too cool to enjoy it* thing. The faux disinterest that he'd thought was so alluring when he'd first started responding to the overtures of women when he was younger. At first, the competitive side of him got off trying to please the beautiful, older women; the lazy way they pulled themselves out of bed buck naked and went to refix their faces. It had felt very…worldly. And he'd gone out of his way to get under their skins. To mess their perfect make-up right up. To be the kind of lover they couldn't just walk away from without a wobble in their step, at least. He'd worked like a dog, becoming technically talented, trying to eke a hint of actual emotion from women who'd made it their business to never give an inch.

When he wanted the whole mile.

He'd always wanted more than people wanted to give.

But buying it…that was a different story.

Izzy had no problem letting him know loud and clear that she enjoyed his horizontal talents—very much. And her guileless appreciation had stirred his blood infinitely more than the practised acrobatics of some of the women in his past.

A man liked to see a hint of worship in his woman's eyes.

This one did, anyway.

He got busy generating some of that worship with his mouth and his hands, employing the shadows to their best effect.

Wait… *His woman?*

Two minutes ago he was thinking they'd burn out within a

week. When had he started thinking of Izzy as *his?* When he'd first buried himself deep inside her? When she'd sat across from the review panel and pitched so passionately and courageously for the otter people? Or tonight, when she'd let him between her thighs?

Did it matter? He sure had a healthy dose of the 'mines', now.

For however long it lasted.

Her tongue in his mouth wasn't helping him keep a particularly clear head. Mirroring for him what he'd done to her earlier this evening. Dipping in and out. Teasing him with what might be ahead.

Christ.

'Come on,' he rasped, pulling his lips free.

His place was just across the bridge but it might as well have been back in Melbourne for all the patience he had for the journey. He wanted to be deep inside Izzy again—right now—and up against a famous art gallery was probably not the most respectful way of accomplishing that. He'd done outdoor sex before but not this close to a whole bunch of intensely surveilled buildings.

'Let's finish this at home.'

Harry threw a leg over hers and tugged Izzy back down to the comfortable covers, grinning. 'Looks like you worked off all those noodles.'

Between the sprint back to his apartment and the mattress marathon... 'I sure did.'

His lips started heading for hers.

She twisted away. 'Nope. I've got to get home. Things to do in the morning.'

'I thought you might stay.'

The moments the words were out, he went totally still. And his sudden tension was infectious.

'That's very uncosmopolitan of you,' she joked lightly. To make it easier on both of them.

'Practical necessity. The trains have finished for the night.'

Ah—something deep inside her twisted into a tiny ball—
of course.

'Just returning the favour,' she quipped. 'You couldn't get
out of my flat fast enough the first time we were together.'

Look at them even having a past to reminisce about.

'Maybe you're just seeing that morning through your own
filter,' he suggested.

'What filter?'

'The filter of inexperience. No, don't get all angry,' he
urged as she sat bolt upright. 'You told me it was your first
one-night stand. I didn't want to stick around making you
more uncomfortable.'

Was it healthy for her cheek capillaries to get quite this
much of a workout? First flushed with sex, now with humiliation. 'Whereas you have them all the time, I suppose.'

Although she really didn't want the answer to that.

'Enough to know how it goes, yeah.'

'Should I be grateful that I get to practise the experience
tonight?'

'We're not a one-night stand anymore.'

'Then what are we?'

Shards of uncertainty chased across the backs of his eyes
as he stared. 'We're…comfortable and exciting.'

Ordinarily 'comfortable' would have to be the kiss of death
for a relationship. It was up there with 'nice'. Except Harry
looked pretty relaxed about the idea. And he'd backed it up
with 'exciting'.

Bonus points for that.

She turned back to him. 'How many women have you slept
with, Harry?'

He almost jerked at the unexpectedness of her question but
he didn't shy away from it.

'Quite a few,' he hedged, and while it wasn't an actual
number his answer was, at least, honest.

'What were they like?'

'What, all of them?'

'If you could group them all together. Sum them up.'

Not because she wanted to hear but because she needed to.

He pulled a pile of pillows up behind him and leaned back into them and for a moment she thought he wasn't going to answer.

'I'd have to split them into two groups,' he finally said. 'Early experiences and later experiences.'

You couldn't keep a good systems man down.

She hugged her arms around herself and hoped it looked casual. 'Okay.'

'The early experiences were amazing. Because they were my first, so I was easy to please. But the ones after that, they were—' he frowned '—routine but slick. In all senses of the word.'

Eww...

'So you'll forgive me for struggling to imagine how you could find me "exciting", then.'

Like the slick brigade.

'You're nothing like them. That's the point.'

'So, I'm like the first lot?'

'No.'

'Then what am I?'

Other than killing this embryonic relationship dead with her needy questions.

But while he looked curious about her questions he didn't look horrified by them. In fact he looked as if he'd been asking himself the same thing.

He lifted his eyes from a moment's deep thought. 'You're unique. You're something new for me.'

'Beginning of phase three, maybe?'

She worked hard not to feel at all special about that.

'You're not really my type.'

Oh. 'Thanks very much.'

'Which makes me wonder if I've had my type wrong all this time. Because, like I said, I'm also extremely comfortable around you. I can't explain it. Even at work, half the time I'd stir you up just to get you in my office.'

The intensity grew almost overwhelming and, for the first

time with Harry, she felt like shrinking away from that blazing focus. But before she could, he changed the subject.

'How are you getting home?'

Disappointment would have curdled the noodles if they weren't already half digested. That was the closest they'd come to personal revelation on his side.

Izzy sighed. 'Inconveniently, my chauffeur knocks off at midnight. So the night bus it is.'

He ignored her sarcasm. 'No. Take a taxi.'

'A taxi will be twenty quid.'

'I'll shout you.'

'You already shouted me dinner.'

'You had sex with me. I'm grateful.'

'Yeah, because that was such a chore.'

Parts of her were still throbbing.

'Seriously, Iz, I want you to be safe. Either take the taxi fare or stay until morning. Which, given the time, will be in a couple of hours.'

Stay over...

That hung out there all iridescent and unmissable. She'd have expected the 'bundling her out through the door in a taxi, like some woman he'd picked up in a bar' part, but he'd asked her *to stay.*

'I'm not taking your money, Harry. And I'm not staying until morning,' she added as he opened his mouth for a third attempt. For reasons she didn't begin to understand it felt important to take a backwards step. Even if she didn't want to.

'Then I'm coming with you,' he insisted. 'And I'll spend the twenty quid anyway getting back here. So either you're going to waste my time *and* my money or just my money. Your call.'

'Harry!'

'I couldn't look my sisters in the eye knowing I'd waved you off on the freaking night bus.'

She was lying too awkwardly to fist her hands on her hips so she hoped her pressed lips and glare would speak volumes.

'Fine. I'll take a bloody taxi.'

'Thank you.'

Yeah. The smug confidence of a man who was accustomed to getting his way. Or so he thought.

'But I'm paying for it.'

'Izzy, come on—'

His vanquished wince was almost worth the twenty pounds and whatever dress she'd have to flog online to free up a bit of cash. Though her satisfaction about such a small win was like a butterfly madly flapping away from a tornado.

Futile.

She lay immobile. 'I pay for it or I take the night bus. Those are your choices.'

He released her legs from under his and flopped back onto his pillow.

'Fine.'

Naww… He was quite sweet when frustrated. She pressed her lips to his. 'Thank you for the concern.'

His grunt might have been resignation or disappointment or wry acknowledgement of a round well played.

Either way it made her smile.

If she couldn't have his trust, she'd take his respect.

CHAPTER NINE

'I FEEL LIKE I should be congratulating you on still being able to walk,' Tori said, biting enthusiastically into her breakfast scroll.

'Toz!'

'Well, you were gone for most of the night. And you were only supposed to be dropping him a bottle of bubbly.'

'I think you're spending too much time with Mark and his filthy imagination. We talked and walked and ate Thai food for most of it.'

A quiet voice chimed in from her left. 'Are you forgetting what his appetiser was?'

'Poppy!'

'Well, why tell me if you don't want me to ever mention it again?'

'Because I'd be in breach of the girlfriend code if I didn't share.'

'It's just such a novelty, Iz.' She sighed. 'I'm probably just envious. You're the only woman in the apartment getting any action.'

'I feel confident your brother's dates are seeing as much action as he did in the military.'

'I try not to think about that happening in the apartment, actually. At least he has the decency to keep the juicy details to himself.'

Something tiny inside her wilted. 'You don't want to hear about it?'

Poppy relented. 'Of course I want to hear about it. Repeatedly and in increasing detail. Ignore me, I'm just fractious.'

'Why? You've got rent coming in on the big room now, courtesy of Isaac, who's barely ever in it, your shifts have been okay and your parents haven't been at you in weeks. Life should be good.'

'Life is a barren wasteland. My best years are rushing past me.'

There was a particular poignancy that she recognised in her friend's voice. It was the tone that said, 'I'm joking but I'm not.'

'Lucky you have that seven-day-a-week study habit, then,' Izzy said.

Poppy's grunt was a pretty good imitation of Harry's. 'Don't suppose you'd be interested in lending me Harry? Just once? No strings attached?'

How curious, her body's immediate tension at the thought of Harry with someone else. But they hadn't talked about exclusivity. And why would they when they weren't even a *thing?*

'I didn't think you went for corporate types, Poppy,' she said instead.

'I'm sure you didn't think I had a type at all.'

'I could say the same about both of you,' Tori scoffed.

'Izzy's had three sexual encounters on two occasions. Not a bad average.'

Was it wrong that she felt vaguely proud about it? 'Four, actually.'

Tori's eyes widened, but before she could squeeze a sound out of her gaping mouth someone whistled down to Ignite's alfresco area. All three of them looked up.

'See you all later,' Alex called down. 'I'm heading to bed.'

'Not alone, I'd wager,' Poppy murmured.

'Smile and wave, Pop. Smile and wave.'

They did their best royal cavalcade, only letting their hands fall back to the table when Alex disappeared back into the apartment for the 'evening'. His evening anyway.

'Is he still all arse about?' Tori asked.

'Roams around all night, sleeps all day. He's like a bat.'

'Even so, we still see more of him than we do of you, Toz. What's going on with you?'

'Ugh, I'm sorry,' she moaned. 'I promise I'll be round more. Especially since your latest new flatmate appears to have a worrying paucity of shirts.'

And a great chest to go with it.

Izzy grinned. 'Perhaps we should direct him to the nearest Oxfam bin.'

'I don't much care what Isaac wears as long as he covers up,' Poppy murmured, grumpily.

Izzy popped her last bit of crust into her mouth, then spoke past the crunch. 'It's a whole unexpected plus to having male flatmates. Who knew?'

'No more of that, Iz,' Tori warned. 'You're a taken woman now.'

'I don't think I'd describe myself as taken. Occasionally occupied, perhaps.'

'He asked you around again tonight,' Poppy pointed out.

'That's hardly a proposal.'

'But it's more than casual.'

'Why would someone like him want more than casual? With someone like me?'

'What's wrong with you?' Tori asked. 'I'd do you in a heartbeat and I'm sure Mark would want to watch.' She took a healthy swallow of her coffee then glanced nervously at both of them. 'Kidding.'

'My point,' Poppy continued, 'is that he's good-looking, he cared enough to make you take a taxi, he's clearly into you and he's no longer your boss. A week or a year, it doesn't matter. You have him right here, right now. Enjoy him. And it.'

Why was she overthinking this? She had a tummy full of breakfast, a full day's worth of research ahead of her to keep her mind occupied, and then another date with Harry tonight. After which she would almost certainly be able to mentally cross through a few more numbers in the battered Kama Sutra on the flat's bookshelves.

Even if it did mean limping home in public, certain everyone knew exactly why she was so crippled.

Don't overthink it...

'Okay. Maybe you're right. And speaking of enjoying...
What do you think my chances are of catching that waiter's
eye for another chai?'

'Screw the chai.' Tori grinned. 'I want to hear all about
number four!'

Hard to imagine that Izzy had ever worried they'd not yet had
a date. They'd been together every day since then in some
shape or form. Dinner, breakfast, shopping, movies, the theatre, galleries. Harry had seen more of London in a few weeks
with her than five years under his own steam.

And he'd seen more of Izzy than any other woman in his
past. Full stop.

It was all very unlike him.

'What do you think?' She modelled a vest intricately woven
from what seemed to be threaded diamonds. If not for the fact
it had come from a street market.

'I think you have expensive tastes.'

'Of course I do. I'm a woman of class.'

Mmm. 'So how do you explain me?'

She considered him for moments. 'I really can't.'

Join the club. It was as if an alien had taken over his body.
Not only had she out-survived the single week of good sex
he'd mentally ascribed her, but he'd seen her virtually every
evening for the past three weeks. And not because Izzy was
pushing it. If anything, she seemed to be trying to put the
brakes on a little.

Thank God one of them was able to be a man about this.

Twenty-two dates. Prior to Izzy, his personal best was six
dates with the one woman. And that was not all at once.

And now he was *shopping* with her.

What the hell?

Except, could you really call it shopping if you didn't purchase anything? He was thirty-two years old and he'd never
even been to markets in his life, let alone come away empty-
handed. Izzy seemed to specialise in wandering around dis-

covering things, admiring them with great gusto and then putting them wistfully back.

It was doing his head in.

'Why don't you just buy it?' he asked as she replaced an ornate picture frame she'd just been gushing over.

'It's not the one.'

'The one what?'

'The one I love enough to spend what I've brought with me.'

'How much is that?'

She pulled a single note from her pocket and held it aloft.

'*Ten pounds?* That's it?'

'I'm on a budget.'

'I'd happily buy you all of the things you've looked at today if we could just leave.'

She spun on him and something indefinable blazed in her eyes. But she didn't say a word. It saddened him that she thought he was having a crack. That she might assume he was bored trolling the endless rows of stalls when the truth was very different. He just wanted to be alone with her again. To enjoy her. To put an end to the sad little sag of her shoulders as she had to put things back.

'Let me just buy something for you.'

He'd never realised how instantly gratification came to him courtesy of his platinum credit cards, and the kind of loose change she was sighing over was nothing to him.

Not that she knew that.

If she did, then how would he know why she was in this thing between them?

Patchy crimson bloomed in her cheeks. Like when she'd arrived at his door after the early morning tube dash. '*I* can buy something for me if I need it. Don't worry, I learned this from the master. Window shopping is a family speciality.'

The more he heard about her childhood, the more disconnected he felt from the rest of the world.

'Being frugal?'

'At not buying every little thing that catches my eye.'

Guilty as charged. Clothes, meals, women.

'Besides,' she went on, 'anything here today is likely to be here again next time we come if I get hit with a sudden pang of *non-buyer's* remorse.'

We.

Why didn't that make him more nervous? Why wasn't all of this making him more nervous? Could it just be because dating Izzy was so…easy? And comfortable. And that somehow being with her energised him. Until he couldn't remember what he'd done with his evenings before they started seeing each other.

Seeing each other. Too early to call themselves a couple, right? Too late to call it just sex.

He looked at her sideways to decide how casual he felt about her. The light coming off her swelled up and filled all gaps between his organs.

Yep, way too late.

'Oh, look. It's Toz!'

Izzy raised one long, elegant hand, then tugged him to the left.

The crazy, multicoloured hair he recognised so well flung around as the woman he hadn't seen since the party turned from what she was doing and focused on them both.

'Izzy!' She air-kissed her friend on both cheeks and then turned on him. Would she even recognise him? She had been pretty hammered.

'Toz, you remember Harry? My, um…'

Izzy's eyes flared as she belatedly realised what a trap she'd set for herself, and a disturbing kind of pallor flooded her skin.

Harry stepped in easily, wanting nothing to crease that perfect brow. Ever. Certainly not something as stupid as his insecurities. 'Her boyfriend.'

Izzy's breath sucked in audibly, but Tori covered like the PR pro she apparently was.

'Harry,' she gushed, a speculative twinkle in her eye. 'Lovely to see you.'

Something told him introductions were redundant. That he'd been the subject of a conversation or two between friends.

Or some parts of him had.

'What are you doing here?' Izzy said, regaining a little of her composure.

'I came to check out Lara's lingerie.'

'The new tenant downstairs? How do you know she has a stall here?'

'It's called talking to people, Iz. You should try it.'

Iz. Toz. Pops.

Harry looked from one to the other. 'Do any of you go by your real names?'

'Alex does,' Tori defended. 'Besides, it's a badge of honour to be granted a nickname.'

He'd been around to Izzy's place a half-dozen times. 'I look forward to the day I get one, then.'

'You already have one,' Tori blurted. Izzy's eyes rounded wildly and, for the first time, Tori looked genuinely apologetic. 'You know…kind of.'

But he kept his focus firmly on Izzy. 'I have a nickname?'

'It's just a silly thing,' she defended, terribly. 'Something fun.'

He kept right on staring. 'I like to have fun.'

Like this. Making two friends squirm for a moment. Evening up the gender imbalance.

'It's…' Izzy almost seemed pale, and he suddenly wondered if maybe it wasn't so fun, after all. 'I'm sure you've had it before.'

And now he was genuinely intrigued. 'Tell me and we'll know.'

'Um…'

Had he ever seen Izzy completely lost for words? Normally she was lightning fast with a comeback.

'Prince Harry,' Tori finally blurted, putting them all out of their misery.

Something tightened up uncomfortably deep inside and he struggled to keep it out of his voice. 'Because I'm freckled and ginger?'

So evidently *not*.

'On account of the great fortune you must have hidden away…' Tori ended on a bit of a fizz '…somewhere.'

Every muscle in his body drew back like a slingshot and an icy calm frosted through him. Beside him Izzy stiffened as she instantly felt his tension.

Awkward silence fell between them all.

'Well, this has gone about as well as the last time we met, Harry,' Tori said brightly, hoisting her parcels more firmly into her arms. 'Whatever will happen next time?'

Out of the corner of his eye, he saw the apologetic glance she shot Izzy as they farewelled each other.

'I'm off to find Lara.'

Izzy's voice was flatter than day-old champagne. 'Bye, Toz.'

'Let's walk,' Harry said.

It was words. Just careless words casually delivered. Tori couldn't know who he was or how well the nickname actually fitted. But the tension remained coiled within him, regardless.

'Prince Harry?'

'Don't be annoyed…' Izzy began, weakly.

Too late. 'From some hidden fortune I supposedly have?'

His jaw was starting to ache. And his head, too, as he saw the confusion and curiosity both blazing in Izzy's eyes. Too much of this and she was going to start asking questions.

Questions he couldn't answer.

'That was just Tori's sense of humour. It was from a long time ago.'

'Your friends didn't know me a long time ago.'

'No, but I did.'

'And?'

'And you weren't always the easiest to get on with.'

'Uh-huh. So you named me after one of the easiest-going royals in history?'

'Oh, for goodness' sake,' she hissed and then spun to face him. 'It's not such a big deal. You lorded it over people back then, but "Lord Harry" didn't have quite the same ring to it. That's all.'

That's all.

So it had nothing to do with fortunes—hidden or otherwise—and everything to do with him being a pain in the arse to work with.

His tension cranked down a few notches.

'Charming.'

'No, we tried Prince Charming and it just didn't quite fit.' Then, when he didn't answer, 'Oh, get over yourself, Harry, it's a nickname. That's all.'

'Did you ever stop to think that maybe I had a reason for doing what I did, Iz?'

How else could he know who he could put his trust in?

Or tell real from fake?

But telling her he was testing people would only lead to more difficult questions he'd be unable to safely answer. The frustration only added fuel to the conversation.

'Is there ever a good reason for being an arrogant jerk?' she challenged.

If he needed any further clues that there was something totally unexpected and new between him and this woman it was this. The fact she could speak to him like that and he wouldn't mind. At all. In fact he appreciated that she just spoke to him straight.

As if he were just anyone.

'You can get the true measure of a person by how they respond under pressure.'

Like this.

Izzy stood her ground. 'Do you know the toll it takes on a person, living with that pressure day in and day out?'

'Yes, actually.' Courtesy of Daddy dearest.

More curiosity streamed in but it was destined to go unfulfilled. Somewhere in the past three weeks, she had learned not to voice the multitude of questions she clearly had about him.

And her very evident resignation on that score made him feel about as worthy as a puppy-kicker.

'And so what do you feel towards that person now? Gratitude for developing your resilience or resentment for making every day a battle?'

A little of both, if he was honest. Which he couldn't be. Not even with her.

What did he feel for his father now? After five years away from his influence and interference?

He released a short breath between his teeth. 'It's complicated.'

Again with that strange, intense look. 'I'm getting the sense lots of things in your life are.'

Not that I'd know.

He'd swear that was what she muttered under her breath as she turned and resumed their stroll. Looking for all the world as if they were just having a regular conversation, not stumbling out of a minefield.

He shook his head, baffled, and trailed her closely as they worked their way through the thickening market crowds. 'Why are you even with me, Izzy? If I caused you that much distress?'

Her face screwed up a little. 'Because you're different when you're not on my case. You're clever and insightful and easy to be around. I like off-duty you.'

'You don't think maybe our relationship being different is half on you?'

She turned her surprise up to him. 'I'm not the one who's changed.'

'You don't think?'

'Do you?'

He considered her for moments. 'I had my own nickname for you, Izzy. "Quickdraw".'

Her brow arched. 'The cerebrally challenged cartoon horse? Thanks very much.'

'Quickdraw because you were always so highly strung and fast to take offence.'

'I was not!' Her voice ratcheted up an octave.

Heh. Case in point.

'That minor outburst excepted, you're a different woman now. Relaxed, chilled out. Why is that?'

She could hardly blame it on him not being around any more.

'Regular sex?' She shrugged.

'You're under more financial pressure than you were before, and more professional stress servicing your new client base. You should be a basket case. Why aren't you?'

'Because…I'm freer. Happy?'

'Is that a question or an answer?'

'I like what I do, now.'

'Why?'

'The obvious things: my hours are up to me, my choices are up to me, my clients are up to me. For the first time.'

'Nothing else?'

Silence fell around them as her hair fell around her face when she was making love on top. Like a private little cocoon. She let the silence grow as they walked. Harry gathered her hand up in his and tugged her closer to him.

'Have I upset you?' he ventured, certain he'd gone too far.

Her face screwed up again. Izzy's concentration face. 'No. But you've made me think. Now I'm trying to figure out exactly when I stopped being happy. And why I didn't notice. I was ecstatic when I went to Trenton, and then uni. I finally had the life I'd always wanted.'

'Maybe you didn't set your childhood goals high enough. Maybe a steady job and a full fridge weren't all that you thought they were going to be?'

She turned bleak eyes up to him. 'But that was everything to me. I gave things up for that.'

What things? he wondered, feeling no small relief that he wasn't the only one keeping secrets.

The shadows behind her eyes dug straight in between his ribs. But not because bad stuff had happened to her, though it had. More because those simple words dripped with self-blame.

'Hindsight is twenty-twenty,' he murmured.

How much could he tell her?

'I've walked away from a thing or two in my life,' he finally said, curling his hand through hers.

Her whole body changed shape as he offered her another titbit from his past. Just scraps, really, but she practically fell on them and he felt like even more of a jerk. She deserved to know everything.

Screw it.

He could just turn to her and tell her, right now, while they were already speaking seriously.

Actually, Iz, there's something you need to know...

He took a deep breath, ready to just blow all his past caution out of the water. Practically buoyant with relief.

'I didn't know what to call you with Tori,' she blurted.

The confession died on his tongue. 'I noticed.'

'You called yourself my...'

He hedged, unaccountably nervous to even use the B-word aloud again. Because of the power that gave her.

'I registered you with building security,' he sidestepped.

Her beautiful eyes flared. 'Did they have to write up the margin-edge to fit me on?'

'Hand on heart, Izzy. I've never put anyone else on the door.'

And he could leave it right there, leave her with that hopeful gleam at the backs of her eyes. Except it wasn't in his nature to be anything but honest. With one glaring and increasingly awkward exception. 'Everyone else had to buzz up.'

A half-dozen people turned their way as Izzy's beautiful laugh ricocheted off the old market walls. 'Thank you, Harry. I think.'

'Not saying it can't be undone. You know, if you start getting difficult to manage.'

Her pretty jaw dropped open. 'To *manage*?'

'When you start getting high maintenance.'

But she was totally up for a bit of verbal foreplay. Of course she was; she was Izzy. 'I'm flattered you think that I haven't yet started.'

He slung his arm around her as they commenced walking again. 'Remember, I've seen Quickdraw in full flight.'

'Fighting words, Mitchell. Do you really want to invoke the P word?'

'I don't mind being your prince, actually. It's healthy to reinforce our comparative social stations.'

Her eyes glittered enticingly. 'You being so far up the mid-management food chain and all?'

He'd been so close just a moment ago.

But if he had told Izzy, how would he ever be certain that she was interested in him and not his name and what came with it? *He* wanted to be responsible for that appreciative gleam in her eyes right now, or for the gasp as his fingers learned her body. Even for the more complex and intriguing hope-filled look she failed to hide from him now and then.

Him.

Not Harrison bloody Broadmore.

And it wasn't enough knowing that she'd entered into a relationship with Harry Mitchell. He wanted her to *stay* in it because of him.

Was 'girlfriend' not going to be enough with this woman?

And just like that Izzy got a second promotion in as many minutes. Most of which she'd spent insulting him. Who would have thought he'd find that appealing?

But those vulnerable moments when she let him in, he lived for those. And every sass she shot at him made him twitch with interest. Which pretty much meant he was walking around with a permanent erection these days.

Twenty-two days seemed a ridiculously small sample on which to be basing something this momentous, but he'd known her a lot longer than that. Sleeping with her that first time had hardly needed a decision; he'd been wanting to taste her for twelve months.

Maybe he'd grown too accustomed to immediate gratification.

Or maybe he just knew right when he felt it.

And he was about to screw that up with a spontaneous confession in the middle of a public market where she'd be totally unprepared for the information? But of course that brought with it the tricky little issue of when *was* a good time. How long would be long enough? A couple of months? A year?

Exactly what kind of a timeline did you put on trust?

They moved towards the ornate market exit and Harry bent to speak more closely to her ear. Desperate to put things back on a footing that he best understood. Comfortable and exciting.

Uncomplicated.

'If I dress up as Prince Harry tonight, what will you wear?'

That was definitely a smile she was struggling to hide. 'My regular clothes.'

'Well, that's dull. How about a wench outfit at least?'

'I lack the cleavage for a convincing wench.'

'Lady of the Lake? That diaphanous, wet shift...'

'Are you turning kinky on me, Harry?'

How was it possible for a single sound to wind back the clock? To erase past hurts and heal over old scars? Yet Izzy's gentle larksong laugh seemed to have that peculiar side-effect. It anchored him in the here and now and it made him start looking forward—where he never looked except to think about his career.

'Just so you can ruin it, tearing it off?' she teased. 'I don't think so.'

'I put you on the register,' he reminded her.

And that wasn't nothing. Not in his world.

'Tell you what,' she compromised. 'If you happen to have some kind of princely attire lying around that draughty tower of yours, I'd be prepared to swoon a little and need to be carried to the sofa.'

And they both knew the amazing things that happened on that sofa.

'You're on.'

CHAPTER TEN

'I THINK YOU'RE imagining things, Izzy.'

'It was him. I swear.'

'Maybe he's a fellow Royal Shakespeare aficionado. London's full of them.'

'And is London full of Portishead fans because I know I saw him at their reunion gig, too. The man from your building.'

Something closed down in Harry's face. 'Coincidence.'

'This is London,' she pushed. 'Eight million people. Coincidences don't happen here.'

'Well, he's gone now, so you can relax.'

Relax. Right. While that whole waiting-for-the-shoe-to-drop thing whooshed around in her brain. Every day she spent with Harry, the sensation intensified. Like something was not quite…right.

'How did you get opening-night seats?' Izzy asked as they left the art deco West End theatre. 'It's been sold out for ever.'

'A friend in the business.'

That was right up there with, 'It's not what you know, Izzy…' And the classic hedge, 'A man never reveals his dating secrets.'

Sheesh—who did a girl have to sleep with to get trusted around here?

Trying to tease some truths out of Harry had stopped being fun weeks ago. She'd never before met anyone who was quite so good at saying nothing. Nothing meaningful, anyway. He was tighter than a drum when it came to any but the most general facts about his life and every time he vagued out on some detail about his life, it left the distinct odour of *intention.*

As though it wasn't necessary to share himself with her.

Because she wasn't going to be around for long. Or because she wasn't worthy.

Or a little from both columns.

Not that she wasn't grateful for the acrobatic sex life. And not that she wasn't thrilled at her growing list of 'done that' fine restaurants and London sights. And she could really grow used to not having to move money around between her credit cards to pay for something.

Mostly she was annoyed because she was *investing* in Harry. She'd taught him to appreciate the wonders of the London transport system. He'd shared his morning boat for one with her and she'd gone along just for the pleasure of seeing his hair get all mussed up on deck before rumpling up his expensive suit a little with her kisses and tubing it back home again. She'd dragged him along on a mini-break up to Scotland to meet her new clients that he'd predictably dubbed 'the Puffin people'.

Yet, despite all his mystery and in spite of all the caginess, Harry still seemed hungry to fill the space she was trying hard to give him—them—and there was a level of intensity to the time they spent together that she'd never experienced before.

Again—as if he knew it wasn't going to last.

And so, every step he came closer, she took a small one back.

Letting herself fall for him wasn't an affordable luxury. Like most of the things in her life now. Yes, he was fabulous. Yes, he was a man she could reasonably expect to be equal with and, yes, the sex was compelling, but if he couldn't share with her there must be a reason.

Was he neck deep in organised crime?

Did he have a wife and family back in Australia?

Witness protection?

Until she'd worked out what that reason was, then her priority had to be protecting herself. Which meant while he rigidly avoided discussing the past, she steadfastly refused to talk about the future.

End result? They both spent a lot of time talking about right now.

The growing animosity between Poppy and their new roommate, Isaac. Tori's ongoing dramas with Mark. Alex's latest shenanigans.

Occasionally Harry would talk about a work problem or a friend she didn't know, but he never talked about his family and if she asked he always answered in the most careful terms. Almost scripted.

Which brought her full circle to just not quizzing him anymore.

A girl could only take so much emotional rejection.

'Mine?' he asked. 'Or yours?'

Which really meant 'sex or no sex?' Harry's bed was the size of the living room at the fire station. And so amazingly comfortable. And it came with a life-sized hot-water bottle in the form of a radiating man.

And no one did naked heat quite like Harry.

She adored him extra much for the fact that 'no sex' was an okay answer. Spooning him to sleep might not be the fastest way to a happy ending for her heart, but nothing made her sleep as deeply as when she was wrapped around Harry's hot back.

Tonight, though, she needed the distraction and the physical workout of hot 'n' heavy with Harry infinitely more than the metronomic rise and fall of his ribs against her skin. Because nothing made her feel more worthy and more certain of their future than that moment when Harry filled every cranny of her body.

And denial was such a warm and cosy place to be.

'Yours,' she sighed.

Sex. The great equaliser.

Was it enough? No. Was it something?

Yes.

Something that needed no discussion between them, no interpretation. And it came with no agenda. It was just good.

Really good.

'Are you purring?' he queried as she guided him onto the underground at Oxford Circus.

She cleared her throat as she shook her head. 'Something caught...'

No. She'd been gurgling with anticipation. She just hadn't meant to do it out loud.

She made it her business to grind back into him much more than was necessary as he wrapped her in the protective circle of his arms during the four-stop run to Vauxhall. His half grin told her he knew exactly what she was doing, but he certainly didn't protest. On the contrary, he held up his end several times by feeling her up in the dim, blown light patches of underground tunnel.

Whether the other train passengers hanging from overhead handles were fooled was anyone's guess.

She felt sure it wasn't the first dry hump ever performed on the underground.

They tumbled through the train's doors the moment they opened and then practically ran to the escalators. People who didn't know how to keep left blocked their way so they couldn't dash up two steps at a time and had to wait, patiently, barely touching each other until the moving stairs tipped them off at the top.

More running, more waiting—this time at traffic lights—and then some forced decorum in the foyer of Harry's building and then, *finally*, they were alone.

Too bad if the lift had CCTV.

Harry practically fell on her the moment the doors closed. Sadly, eight floors was hardly enough to get any serious action happening, but he managed to squeeze in some serious groping and a lot of kissing before the doors opened again on the penthouse level.

'Keys...' he murmured against her lips and she fished his keys and phone from her bag.

That was a thing they did now, too. She carried some of his stuff. So, she was taking her intimacies where she could get them.

And then they were in, back amid the luxury and privacy of his apartment. Somehow he managed to keep the contact between their skin even as he shed layers of clothing onto the plush carpet.

Izzy thought about all the talking she'd wanted to do. All the emotional closeness she'd wanted to work on. A foundation on which she could feel confident about their relationship…if that was what this truly was. Questions she could ask him that might not get caught up in his personal spam filter for secrets.

I'm not looking for a relationship, he'd warned that first time they were together.

Rubbish. Everything about his behaviour towards her since then said he was crying out for a relationship. For someone to keep close, to confide in, to share with. And everything seemed to indicate that *that someone* was her.

Everything except the secrecy, that was.

What aren't you telling me, Harry?

His mouth ravaged her throat and it seemed designed to distract her from even her thoughts. Should she be more upset with him or with herself that she was so easily turned from purpose?

Her head tipped back to give him access to that special place they both loved best. The place that only he knew kindled her fires better than anything else. Who else was she ever going to find who could know her body so damned well? Who could play it like a fine instrument.

No one. Harry was it.

Her heart missed a beat. Possibly two.

Oh, crap.

Despite everything she'd done to keep herself at arm's length she'd started to fall for Harry. She let those little moments of kindness or sweetness or gentleness wiggle under her skin and do their subtle work. All the days she spent with him, all the nights, weren't just about getting to know him. Or him getting to know her. She was there because it just felt *wrong* not to be. To know Harry and not be with him.

It would be like finding the part of herself she'd been looking for all this time and then just casually throwing it away.

But she was raised a survivor. If Harry couldn't bring himself to open up by himself then she'd raise it before they went
any further.

Enough was enough.

'Harry...' she breathed, pulling back just slightly from him.

But then his mouth found the breast that was practically
afire from all the casual brushing on the tube and he sucked
and nipped all that determination straight from her head.

'Oh, sod it,' she whispered.

Tomorrow.

'Holy Christ, this was not a good idea...'

Tori doubled over, pressing a hand into her side and heaving great sucks of air into her lungs.

'Maybe if you ran more than once every six months it
wouldn't be such a challenge,' Poppy pointed out.

'Maybe if I had breast reduction it wouldn't be such a challenge,' she quipped. 'I'm going to knock myself senseless if
I'm not careful.'

Izzy slid down onto the bench next to her, only half listening.

'Earth to Izzy?'

Her head snapped up.

'Jogging is your cone of silence,' Poppy pointed out. 'You
only bring us when you have an upper case I issue to work
through. So spill. What's up?'

'I'm comfortable and exciting,' she said with no benefit
of introduction.

'Is that a general affirmation—' Tori frowned '—or are
we talking about Harry?'

'Harry.'

Her friends glanced at each other.

'Well, exciting is good.' Tori nodded. 'And comfort is...
valuable. It gives you something solid to fall back on when
the excitement wanes.'

There was an optimistic thought.

'No, I mean why is he with me? There must be plenty of "exciting" women available to a man like him.'

And even more comfortable ones.

Tori plonked down next to her. 'A mid-level manager at a conservative finance firm isn't exactly fishing out of your league, Izzy.'

'No. I guess…'

'What?' Poppy's eyes narrowed. 'I know that lip-gnaw anywhere.'

Sure enough the inside of her cheek had found its way between her canines. 'He's…I think there's more to him than you might suspect.'

'I knew it! Hung like a camel, right?'

'Tori!' Her energy drink ended up half dribbling down her chin. 'I can't put my finger on it. He's just…secretive.'

Poppy instantly sobered. 'He's not married, is he?'

'No.'

Tori leaned in and lowered her voice. 'Did he try your underwear on?'

'What? No!'

Tori tossed her hair back, eyes darting around. 'No. Right. Mark never did either.'

But the way she slumped down on the bench and became instantly fascinated with her laces told a very different story.

'Look,' Poppy sighed. 'He's gainfully employed, he's good-looking, he's straight and he makes sure you climax first. I think you can credit him a secret or two until you get to know each other a bit better.'

'Unless it's the underwear,' Tori murmured.

'Or the wife,' Poppy added.

'He's not married or a cross-dresser.' Izzy frowned. 'When does a "secret" become a lie?' she asked.

Tori grew more serious than Izzy had ever seen her. 'When it starts hurting you.'

Izzy's gaze dropped to the footpath and she started to speak and then stopped. Why? These were her closest friends. If she couldn't be honest with them, then who?

'I don't always feel good about myself when I'm with him,' she finally admitted.

Neither woman had anything clever to say about that.

At all.

'Why, Iz?'

She shook her head. 'It's hard to explain.'

'Do we look like we're ready to be running again?'

'He's so giving, physically, and generous with his time and money...'

'But?'

'But he doesn't give of himself. I know all these things about him as a person but nothing concrete. I know that he went to boarding school but not where or when. I know he has sisters but not how many or who they are. I know he's from Australia but I know nothing about his life there. Like he doesn't want me to know.'

'Oh-h-h...' Poppy murmured.

'Or that I'm not going to be around long enough for it to matter.' She sighed. 'I live with this vague feeling that I'm batting way above my average with him.'

'Isadora Dean!' Poppy scolded. 'You are plenty good enough for any man.'

'I assume you've checked him out online?' Tori asked out-right.

Izzy lifted her heard. 'That's a bit creepy, isn't it?'

'Are you kidding? Basic dating due diligence. I'm not say-ing stalk the guy, just check out his footprint. Get the basics. Maybe that will help you understand him.'

'It just feels wrong.'

'Then ask him outright.'

'What if I'm too scared of the answer?'

Silence stretched out. And out. All the endorphins from their run lay scattered in ruins around their feet.

'Is this about your family, Iz?'

And by 'family' Poppy meant 'childhood'.

Isadora couldn't be poorer...

'No, it's—' But what exactly was it, then? 'I just know that everything he doesn't say has a lot more power over me than the things he does. I find them impossible to ignore. And the good things impossible to trust.'

Poppy gnawed her lip. 'I thought he was treating you like a princess.'

'He is. In some ways. He's just not open.'

'Iz,' Tori started. 'Normally I'd say that kind, handsome men who press you against art gallery walls and kiss you senseless don't come along every day. That you should give him a chance.'

A chance…hadn't her reasonable side said much the same thing?

'But, if you don't feel good about yourself now, after just a few weeks with him, where will you be in five years?'

A desperate kind of sadness washed over her, that Tori had summarised her tragedy so succinctly.

'I really want this to work out,' she whispered.

Poppy wrapped an arm around her shoulder. 'I know, love.'

Tori pushed to her feet and pulled Izzy up behind her. 'Come on. I think this is a job for SupperMan.'

The best cakes in Notting Hill. Izzy tugged her emergency twenty pounds out of her running bra.

'No, this one's on me, Iz.' She turned to Poppy. 'Chocolate cake, Dr Spencer. Stat!'

'And you know what goes perfectly with chocolate cake?' Tori added, curling her arm through Izzy's. 'Google.'

He should have followed through that day at the markets.

Told Izzy everything.

If he had he wouldn't be facing the gut-churning reality that he couldn't take their relationship further until he'd fessed up. Who he was. Why he'd been lying.

That he'd been lying.

It seemed foolish now not to have told her right back in their first week, before the telling carried so much extra weight even if the words themselves were weightless. There must have been a point weeks ago when he'd decided she was going to be in his life for longer than a week—two weeks, three—that his brain should have nudged him to confess. Back when the deception was only young.

Now it was fully grown. Hell, it practically had grown up kids of its own. Telling Izzy now that he'd been lying to her for every one of thirty dates—thirty hot nights and hotter mornings—was going to be brutal.

That was a long time to not tell someone something so fundamental.

And he'd deserve every bit of the recriminations she'd throw at him. He had to assume that she'd go ballistic. He would, if it was his trust being betrayed.

But it wasn't the worst news in the world, right? Especially for someone who was a card-carrying fan of cash. It wasn't as if he were dirt poor and pretending to be rich.

Hey, good news, Iz. I'm loaded!

She'd jump up and down as if she'd just won the lottery. And they'd all live happily ever after. The end.

Assuming she didn't slap his face and walk out.

Which was a distinct possibility.

But Izzy was nothing if not a realist. He'd explain that he'd wanted to wait until their relationship was more certain before telling her and then he'd struggled to find the right time. And a month wasn't really that long to be vacillating, right?

Sure, an annoying little voice said, *if you were going by the calendar.* If you were going by the number of dates or conversations or intense sexual experiences they'd had it was near criminal. Some people didn't experience that much in a year.

Some people didn't experience it in their whole lives.

A lifetime with Izzy, the idea felt nothing but…right.

Isadora Dean was not his mother. And what a freaking relief it was to discover that he was categorically not his father. He and Izzy were having a perfectly functional, perfectly healthy, perfectly *perfect* relationship.

Well, not quite *perfect*, but he'd fix that as soon as she walked in tonight.

Full disclosure. Full explanation.

With a surprise chaser.

He patted his pocket. Not what he'd gone out for today but the moment he held it in his hand everything in his world just clicked into place. Even the London light got brighter.

The lift dropped him up on his floor and the guy from two doors down was standing in the hallway looking intense.

'Hey,' Harry said awkwardly given how long they'd shared this floor. He didn't even know the guy's name.

The man stepped towards him but, just then, his phone rang and the stranger drew back, waiting respectfully. Almost deferentially. Harry threw him a half apology as he fumbled his phone out of his back pocket and pressed it to his ear, entering his apartment.

'Yeh-lo?' he answered absently, closing the door behind him.

On the other end—far on the other end—a female voice burst into tears. He bent his head to try and make sense of the hysterical shrieking.

'Mags…?'

Behind him, the doorbell rang.

'He can't not exist at all, Izzy,' Poppy admonished, reversing out of the kitchen with a tray filled with steaming tea makings.

'He's not on social-media sites, or the professional networks. Plenty of other Harry Mitchells but not him.'

Not *her* Harry.

'Try the video sites,' Tori suggested. 'He must have at least stuck a pair of carrot sticks up his nose and filmed it at some point in his life. That's a rite of passage, isn't it?'

Izzy flopped back onto the sofa. Lord, how did people manage before the internet? Back in the Dark Ages. But it didn't take long to rule that out, either…

'Nothing. I just can't find him.'

And her Izzometer spun even more wildly.

'Broaden your search,' Alex muttered as he returned from the bathroom in his boxers, his face sleep creased. Tori's lips split into an enormous smile at the sight of a semi-naked hard body in the room.

Poppy just rolled her eyes. 'Brilliant tech support, Alex, thank you.'

He waved two fingers. 'I'm going back to bed, then. Night.'

'Afternoon!' Poppy called.

Tori craned her neck for one last look as he marched away.

Izzy tabbed the cursor back to where she'd written *Harry Mitchell* and added *Broadmore Natále* for good measure. If this was a money trail she was trying to find and not a person she'd start with the confirmed knowns. Name and occupation.

Google immediately knew better.

Did you mean Harrison Mitchell Broadmore? it asked.

'Not really,' she muttered, irritated, her finger hovering over her original search, ready to override the computer brain. But then it hit her: maybe Harry really was short for something like Harrison?

She clicked yes. Why not?

Dozens—hundreds—of results streamed down for Harrison Mitchell and Broadmore. Images, news reports, gossip articles. The works.

Someone was a busy boy.

She clicked through image results for some big New York masters of the universe corporate gathering until she paused on a familiar, lined face. Weston Broadmore, founder of the firm she'd so recently stuck one finger up at. One or two of him with what could only be called his trophy wife. Mostly breast. And everything that wasn't breast was blonde. And young. Really, quite young compared to Broadmore's seventy-plus years.

But…they were still together and both on their only marriage. And that was something in this day and age. Must be love.

She clicked the next image result and hit an older shot, a

less-grey version of Broadmore, ushering a gaggle of teenaged children into a stadium. All girls but one.

The Broadmore brood, the caption read. Carla, Margaret,
Kathryn and Harrison.

Nice-looking girls—or they would be by now. Nice-looking
boy, too. Little. No more than ten. Their father had a slightly
harassed look on his face and the hand urging his son forward
looked impatient. In return, the kid was glancing up at him
with a conflicted twist on his little lips.

Wait…

Izzy squinted and scrolled the image bigger. Zooming right
in on that little face as the hairs on her neck sprang to attention. Why did that sardonic grimace look so familiar? A
baby…admittedly…but familiar.

She redid the web search to remove *Mitchell* from the mix
and the list of results refined dramatically.

Harrison Broadmore, captured in Australia a dozen years
ago. Dressed for the beach. Cap down low over his eyes. Nice,
stubbled jaw visible below it. Amazing young torso below
that. Her whole body responded before she could think about
the inappropriateness of her nipples tightening for a teenager.

She focused on hunting further.

Click. Click. Cli—

Her finger froze, suspended over the keypad, eyes glued
to her laptop's screen, which displayed a more professional
photo of a more professionally presented Broadmore heir. In
a suit, like his father. And recent. She let the finger fall gently
onto the screen. Resting it over Harrison Broadmore's heart.

Using it as an anchor to stop the wild thrumming of her
own.

Not Harrison Mitchell *and* Broadmore.

Harrison Mitchell Broadmore.

Harry.

Corporate to the max, but one hundred per cent *her* Harry.

Her stomach rolled. Was this what he'd been keeping from
her? The reason for all the caginess and ambiguity and his
aversion to media attention? Had he been working his way up

through departments in one of Broadmore's subsidiary firms? Was it some kind of hidden camera *Undercover Boss* thing for television? Or had he gone rogue, and his family didn't even know where he was as some of the websites suggested? Or was this some kind of hilarious incognito experiment rich people liked to conduct?

A dozen questions swamped in at once and pressed down onto her roiling stomach but they all pointed the same way.

Harry Mitchell and Harrison Broadmore were the same man.

And they were both liars.

Every time he didn't tell her the truth. Every time she gave him one of her quizzical looks and he distracted her with a kiss.

Lying. And rich.

And lying about being rich.

All the while shagging her senseless.

Why? Did he prefer his sexual activity to be confidential? He was already taking her to top restaurants and entertainment—did he imagine she'd want more? Did he think she'd demand to be part of his celebrity world, if she knew?

That set her off in a fury of searching and, sure enough, the internet was clogged with images of a younger him mixing it up with celebrities and gazillionaires alike.

And women... So many women...

She swallowed back a soggy lump and forced herself onwards.

Only a handful of images from the past few years, and a few 'What's happened to Harry?' type blog pieces trying to dig up his whereabouts. So his lying was purely a UK thing, then?

Lucky England.

No wife, her subconscious urged. *No organised crime.* That was something, right?

He was just rich.

Rich. Four little letters.

Four little letters and a few minutes on her laptop and

Harry suddenly became her 'better'. The exclusive privacy of the places he took her to eat made her feel suspicious, not special. The exciting foreplay up against the Tate and on the tube suddenly smacked of slumming when viewed through a money-coloured filter.

Because it was no longer between two people who were each other's equal. Two people who were enjoying exploring and getting to know each other. Two people just caught up in an unexpected affair.

Harry was heir to one of the top fortunes in the corporate world.

She was a nobody from the Chorlton estates who slept in a closet.

'Did you find him, Iz?'

Poppy's voice was an indistinct blur amid her wildly spiralling thoughts. Impossible to marshal once they were whipped up into a dread-based frenzy.

Every fear she'd ever harboured warred with her sense of natural justice. She couldn't condemn the man before giving him half a chance, right? And there were no relationship rules stipulating a timeframe for full disclosure. Harry might have had a really good reason not to tell her who he really was before now.

Like…

She sat there staring at her laptop screen, thinking. And she got nothing. Nothing but the witness protection thing.

There was only one way to find out—a crazy, novel thought.

Ask him… Like a grown-up, and then deal with what came. That was what brave Izzy would have done. Brave, idealistic Izzy.

Or—logical, unflappable Izzy reasoned—*you could give him a chance to tell you off his own bat.* Be available. Be willing to hear. Be calm and mature and modern about it. Let it come.

See if he tells you at all, whispered burned, cynical Izzy.

'He will,' she said aloud, shaking her computer just slightly.

And soon.

'Who will what?' Tori frowned.

She refreshed the page and selected the top news story, the one from two hours ago.

Harry...!

Poppy cried out as Izzy shot to her feet and sent her computer flying into her friend's lap.

'I have to go…'

She snatched her phone from the table, shoving it into the accessory pocket of her running pants, and sprinted for the door. Behind her, Tori reached for the laptop as Poppy gaped.

'What—?'

'I have to go!'

CHAPTER ELEVEN

'PLEASE, CAN YOU drive any faster?'

'This is London, love, not Monaco,' the taxi driver commented. 'I go as fast as the traffic allows.'

Izzy took pity on her inner cheek and gnawed on her fingernail instead. It seemed to help with the interminable drive across town.

'I'll jump out here, thanks,' she said, knowing it was probably quicker to jog on foot through the bikeways and private lanes down to the embankment than to sit here in the taxi observing the niceties of the peak-hour road rules.

She tossed the driver her emergency twenty from her bra and sacrificed the change as she slammed the door behind her. Her long legs carried her down the rear lane of endless residential buildings, through parks and between the creeping traffic towards Vauxhall Bridge. Boom gates and no-entry signs meant nothing just now. It occurred to her, vaguely, that some of those no-entry laneways probably belonged to MI5, but hopefully all they'd see on their security monitors was a young woman out for a jog and taking a few unsanctioned short cuts.

Her runners ate up the last five hundred metres of the bridge and Riverside Walk and she arrived, gasping for breath, at the glamorous Thameside entry to Harry's sprawling complex.

Thank God for the register. It meant only the barest pause to announce herself to the security, who were too polite to so much as lift an eyebrow at her casualwear and flushed face. And thank God for the mirrored walls of the lift, which let her remedy the worst of the damage to her face and hair.

The lift opened on the top floor just metres from Harry's apartment and she fell on his door, leaning hard on the bell.

Harry opened it almost immediately, shadows under his beautiful eyes, and paler than his lifetime tan should have allowed. His face transformed from grief to something blazing and bright as she fell into his arms. They slid up around her and held on as if she was the one giving him strength.

She practically willed some into him.

'You came,' he breathed against her neck.

'Your father!' she gasped, still struggling for air. 'I'm so sorry. What can I do?'

His entire body locked up hard, except those parts he needed to push her slightly away. Apparently his Australian tan *could* get paler. 'What?'

'I read about his heart attack online. Are you going home? What do you need?'

The shock slowly morphed into something else. Something edgy and unfamiliar. 'My father?'

'Weston Broadmore,' she explained in case he was in some kind of shock from the news. But that wasn't shock on his face, she finally realised, it was anger.

A rigid kind of anger.

A man exited the second lift behind her. The man from Portishead. And Shakespeare. And Harry's building. Harry caught his eyes and acknowledged him with the briefest of nods.

'Do you really want to talk about this out here?' she puffed.

He stepped aside and she practically tumbled into the comfortable apartment.

He spun on her. 'You know?'

She waved away his concern and crossed close to him and curled her fingers around his arm. 'What can I do, Harry?'

He didn't yank his arm away but the frozen way he stood was almost worse. 'Nothing.'

'So you're going home?'

'Of course.'

His icy tone muddled her already racing mind. 'Yes, sorry. Dumb question.' She squeezed his arm again. 'How is your father?'

'Dying.'

Icy *and* little better than monosyllabic. It finally got her attention. She stepped back and peered up at him. 'Are you okay?'

'Well, my father's in critical care…'

'I mean, are you okay *with me?* You seem angry.'

'What gave me away?'

Sarcasm had always been his sharpest tool. The unfairness of that bit deep inside. 'I've just run across half of London to be here for you.'

'If you'd run just a bit slower you'd have missed me.'

Her eyes fell on the two packed bags by his feet. And on the man waiting politely in the hall.

Now? He was going right now? A wild panic started building in her gut. 'I'll come with you to Australia.' That was what credit cards were for, right? Emergency transcontinental flights. 'We'll just need to stop by the—'

'I hope you're not expecting me to pick up the tab?'

His blunt tone had her taking a step back from him. In all his many guises, she'd never heard Harry be outright nasty. Or snarky about her lack of funds. Though a tiny voice reminded her that she really wouldn't know what Harrison Broadmore was like at all.

'No, I…'

But her airways weren't clear all of a sudden. There was that feeling again, the whole he-makes-me-feel-bad-about-myself thing. Amplified times ten. She pressed shaking fingers to her sternum.

His face twisted for a half ¨umoment but then steadied. He shuddered in a breath. 'How long have you known who I am?'

She rushed to reassure him. 'I'm not upset. I figured you'd tell me when you were ready.'

'*You're* not upset? Oh, good.'

'Harry, do you really want to talk about this now?'

'You've been lying to me, Izzy!'

Old wounds stretched their scars at the flat-out judgement in his tone. Guilty until proven innocent.

But it wasn't *her* father lying in a hospital halfway around the world, and, now that she knew who that father was, Harry had to be facing a world of new pressure. Sisters. A mother. A global corporation. Responsibility she could barely conceive.

She was the one who needed to suck it up, right now. Be the grown-up.

She took a deep breath. 'Let's talk about this when you get back.'

Not that she wanted either of them stewing on the hurtful accusations of the past few minutes, but he wasn't thinking clearly now. And her own adrenaline was so high she was liable to say something she'd regret.

'I'm unlikely to be back,' he said. Flat. Dead. Uninterested.

Her knees wobbled dangerously, the shock and latent lactic acid from her sprint doing their job together. 'What?'

'I had to go home eventually. My father's heart attack has just brought that forward.'

'You're never coming back? At all?' she whispered. And then something else occurred to her. 'Were you going to let me know?'

Or was it just one of the many things he'd decided not to tell her?

'I called you.'

As he spoke realisation flooded into his eyes and they flared wide for a moment. 'When you hear it you can disregard the whole message.' Intensity blazed. 'All of it.'

'So…that's it? We're done?'

'Disappointed, Izzy?'

She pushed out words between the sharp ache. That he'd even have to ask. 'Yes. Of course.'

Disappointed. Confused. Lost.

Absolutely bloody heart sore.

Here she'd been all primed to work through their communication issues.

'All that effort wasted.'

'What are you talking about? What effort?'

'I have to give you points for your approach. Turning up

at my door with champagne. Half an hour later you had your thighs around my ears.'

'Harry!' She glanced at the open doorway, desperate, mortified. The man in the hall stared at some point on a far wall and pretended not to have heard.

'Truth's ugly from that angle, huh?' He stalked to the far side of the room.

Oh, my God...

'I came here because I thought you'd be devastated about your father. I thought you'd need my support. What is wrong with you?'

He spun back. 'You thought your ship was coming in early, you mean, and you didn't want to miss it.'

Oh, God...the Broadmore billions. Was that what this was about?

'I'm not interested in your money, Harry.'

'I know how this goes, Izzy,' he thundered. 'I've watched this all my life. Beautiful woman uses sex to get what she wants. Well, you can blame my father's dodgy heart and lifetime of excess for cutting you off at the knees. If not for that, who knows what might have happened?'

His face grew even more thunderous and his hands worked furiously in his pocket. At something in there.

'Full credit to you, Izzy. You've done a bang-up job of making yourself feel like part of the furniture in that time. Like you belonged here in my life. You almost had me fooled.'

A discreet throat-clear at the ajar door. 'We need to get going, Mr Broadmore.'

The use of Harry's real name threw her. Especially from another tenant.

Harry reached for his bag. 'I have to go.'

'You'd rather take a lift with a stranger than with me?'

Was he that angry?

'He's my personal guard. He's arranged the jet to get me home.'

An aching numbness surged through her veins. Bodyguards. Private jets. Uber suspicion. Was that the world he really came from? It was more than alien.

It was awful.

She slid her hand over his as it reached for the door. 'You could do that? Just wipe off everything we've had?'

It took him a moment, but he finally turned his face half back to her. 'What have we had, Izzy?'

'Something special. Something unique.'

But as she said the words she realised how ridiculously naïve they sounded. Harry was just an overgrown rich kid killing a few years in London working for Daddy's firm and slumming it with a local. Having some good times. He'd made her no promises, he'd given her virtually nothing of himself, he'd even warned her—multiple times—that all they really had going between them was sizzling chemistry.

Chemistry that, even now, zinged like electricity between them.

'It's not special or unique, Izzy—'

Of course, she heard *'you're not special'* and *'you're not unique'*.

'—it's what I grew up with. And I promised myself I'd never let it happen to me.'

His parents, with their corporate merger of a marriage that was so acrimonious even the internet knew all about it. The model against which Harry must measure all relationships.

Words rushed up her trachea and over her lips. The only thing she could possibly say. An utterly useless thing.

'I love you, Harry.'

Of all the ways she'd thought about confessing it—draped on a petal-strewn bed, standing atop the Eiffel Tower, rugged up by a fire in some cottage in Scotland—standing here dying, moments before never seeing him again, was not one of them.

Part of her wished she were strong enough to stay silent.

He froze with his back to her, halfway to picking up the second suitcase. His voice was thick and measured. 'Just let it go, Iz. You gave it a shot. Retire gracefully.'

'Please don't leave things like this,' she begged.

He reanimated, picked up his bag and turned. 'I have a jet waiting.'

'It's real!' She grabbed his arm. 'I swear.'

He shrugged her off. When he lifted his eyes, his expression—his voice—was devoid of…pretty much everything. '*This* is the first real moment you and I have had together—no secrets, no lies between us—and it's hardly going well, is it?'

He walked through his front door and left it gaping, handing his bag to the dark-suited man standing there. Every bit the CEO in training. The same lift that she'd arrived in opened for him immediately.

Panic twisted through her.

If Harry got on that plane feeling as he did she would never hear from him again. He'd find too many reasons to wipe her from his consciousness. Too many excuses to let it happen.

If anyone knew how easy it was to write off someone you loved it was her.

So, while it galled her to beg, some things were more important than pride.

She started forward. 'Please, Harry—'

He flicked the merest glance to his security, who neatly blocked her with one strong arm across the lift entrance.

'Pull the door shut behind you when you go,' Harry said, bleak and cold. And then, because he couldn't help himself, he added, 'Don't steal anything.'

And then the doors slid shut.

Izzy stumbled back against the foyer wall and collapsed against its solid strength.

What the hell had just happened?

How could he be so angry at her when he'd been the one lying for weeks? Months! She'd been in possession of his secret for less than an hour.

Why didn't she call him on all the secrecy earlier? Or at all. Maybe the only truthful thing he'd said to her was that he wasn't looking for a relationship. But she'd been wilfully blind to it because she'd finally found somewhere she *fitted*.

In Harry Mitchell's arms.

She sacrificed her T-shirt to her tear-streamed face, sliding down the wall into a ball on the plush carpet.

She would never feel this carpet under her bare feet again. She'd never see Harry's particular view or lie on his big, comfortable bed again. She'd never feel his arms around her or his hot, bare chest against her skin, or sit with him in a bad movie and laugh at his lame sense of humour.

She would never taste him, or feel him inside her, or hear his sexy voice.

And she'd never get to ask him *why* he felt the need to lie to the world. To her.

Through the shambles of conflicting thoughts, one phrase cut through.

His voice...

Her tears eased a fraction.

She reached behind her and pulled her mobile from her pocket. It might as well have weighed a tonne for all the strength her fingers had. It took only a second to pick up her voicemail.

'Iz. It's me...I've been called back to Australia effective immediately. Family emergency.' She tried not to respond to the strained anxiety in his voice. *'I don't know when I'll be back. My flight leaves at four. Call me if you get this message in time.'*

That was it.

Not, 'My father's had a heart attack, Iz.'

No, 'I'm going to be lost without you, Iz.'

Absent of, 'I'll miss you, Iz.'

She played the message again. And then again. Nothing about the simple message changed. But on the last play it automatically began the second message in her queue.

'God, sorry...' Just listening to his accent it hurt. *'My head's all over the place. I wanted to see you, but I have to get back for the girls. They're beside themselves. Mum's pretty useless in a crisis and they...'* His sigh was deep and mournful. *'They need their brother.*

'I'll come back to you as soon as I can. There's something

I need to tell you. And something I have for you. Keep me in your thoughts, Izzy. I love you, Quickdraw. I'll miss you.'

Beep.

Something deep in her chest swelled to overflowing. Until it ached. His words were so simple, yet so heartfelt. So rich with frustration and grief and hope and loss. And with love.

Harry Mitchell loved her.

An hour ago, anyway.

The thing spreading in her chest curled back into a tight fist.

When you hear it you can disregard the whole message... All of it.

The flare of panic as he remembered his message, then the dead nothing in his eyes as he'd said those awful words... What did he mean by 'all of it'? The intimate, affectionate tone? The concern for her feelings?

The love part?

What had changed? She'd come to him. She'd *run* to him. Despite all her misgivings about his motives, she went where he needed her. By his side.

She played the message again.

It didn't hurt any less.

But pain was at least better than the big, empty, lonely void she feared she'd be left with where Harry had just vacated.

She lifted the phone again but this time she pressed different keys. Doing something she should have had the courage for much, much sooner.

Her eyes stung as it rang and then they fluttered shut as it answered.

'Mum?' she whispered. 'I need you...'

CHAPTER TWELVE

EVEN THE BEST room in the best Australian hospital was too pedestrian for Weston Broadmore. The moment his father was released from Intensive Care, he relocated, bringing an entourage of nurses and specialists and a swathe of security personnel home with him. The whole upstairs wing now looked like a military operation.

His father was doing okay, but the media were salivating over the story like starved dogs: finance baron irreparably broken, young heir steps out of the shadows to take up the reins. Not that anyone had said that aloud, but the whole world knew that seventy-nine-year-old Weston Broadmore might have survived but wasn't going to be running his company, personally, any longer.

'You look pretty miserable for someone who just inherited a billion-dollar empire.' The soft voice came from behind him in the hallway. He turned into the warm brush of lips on his cheek.

'Carla.' His oldest sister. His favourite.

His role model. The woman who'd overcome a misogynist's ignorance—and his disbelief—to work her way up to a high-ranking job in her father's company.

'This is not how I imagined it all happening,' he murmured, staring into the makeshift triage, where people in blue scrubs buzzed quietly around his father like bees around a queen.

She squeezed his shoulder. 'Your ascension to the throne? How did you imagine it?'

'I was older.' Much older. With a wife and kids. Tall, willowy kids. 'And everyone was much more warm and fuzzy about it all.'

'Warm and fuzzy?' Carla's snort brought one of the nurses'

critical gazes around to where they were standing. 'You did grow up in this family, right?'

'This family is not just about one man any more than this company is. There's plenty of potential for warm and fuzzy in our branch of the family tree.'

Him. His sisters. No shortage of love and loyalty there, even if they'd never really been encouraged to be huggy about it.

'I think you forget who fathered us. And mothered.'

No. It took a special kind of hardness to tie yourself to a man like Weston Broadmore for life. Harry knew how trapped he'd felt his whole life by the weighty expectations on him as heir. And he'd been watching his mother closely since he got back. Looking for signs of relief. Ambition. But only finding pinches of anxiety around her eyes. For her husband or for her future?

'Lord only knows the kind of strength it takes to live in a loveless marriage where your every move is scrutinised.'

Even if you'd engineered it yourself.

Carla stared. 'What did you *do* in London? You've come back quite changed.'

'I watched. And I absorbed. Learned.'

'From who, the Dalai Lama?'

Immediately his mind betrayed him and went straight to Izzy. His gut squeezed.

'You sound just like him.' He nodded towards the shrouded figure at the centre of all the nursing attention.

Carla grimaced. 'God forbid.'

He turned and caught her eyes. 'Listen—'

'Don't. I know what you're going to say.'

'How do you know?'

'Because it's what I'd say if I was in your position. Dragged back from freedom to take the rudder. That you're sorry our father is such a Neanderthal. That you're sorry that he passed over every girl in the family to leave everything to the only boy.'

'I *am* sorry, Carla.'

'I know. Because you're a good person. And because it's not your fault Mum finally managed to make a Y chromosome.'

His eyes fell shut.

'We're proud of you, you know that? Me and Katie and Mags. Dad couldn't see it but I knew what you were doing over there. *We* knew. And we were cheering for you every time you got promoted. On your own. No matter what happens you will always know you earned that fair and square.'

One thing in his life worked out, anyway.

'And Dad will never, ever get it,' Carla went on. 'He'll go to his grave being secretly surprised at the success you're going to make of running the corporation but giving himself all the credit. But you are the man you are *despite* him, not *because* of him. Always believe that.'

He swallowed back any response. With a throat as thick as his and the week he'd just had he was liable to blurt out everything to his big sister. But he curled his fingers through hers and let their firm pressure do the talking.

They went back to watching the medical hustle and bustle.

'Anyway,' Carla sighed deeply, 'I came up here for a reason, Harry. There's someone here for you, in the study.'

He swore. 'Another journalist? Let them wait.'

Carla watched him sideways. 'Someone from the London office. Looking for a handover.'

The same London office that he'd lied to for five years? The London office who'd be thinking back over those years looking for the slightest offences they might be punished for when he took over the big seat. The same London office who'd be struggling right now after a week with no one at the helm of their finance department.

'I guess I owe them that, at least.'

He followed his sister down the ornate, timber staircase and trailed her clicks across the expensive, polished floors. The same floors they used to slide along on pillowcases, back when the pillowcases were bigger than they were. And when both their parents were out.

Carla stopped just short of the study, kissed his cheek and excused herself quietly. 'See you for lunch.'

Everything was whispers. Everywhere in the house.

As if they were mourning in anticipation.

He cleared his throat loudly by way of a butler's introduction and pushed the study door open. Maybe he could get this done in an hour...

His feet stumbled to a halt.

Izzy stood, like some kind of mirage, in the last place he ever imagined seeing her. His father's study. Glancing around at the opulence as if it were a foreign civilisation she'd just uncovered.

Every muscle in his body did the full fight-or-flight clench.

Except for his heart; that swelled to twice its size just for seeing her. In that split second before his mind recalled how he'd been played.

He beat it down with a club.

'Thank you for seeing me, Harry.'

If he'd known it was her he wouldn't have. Betrayal was cancerous enough inside you without having to look it in the eye, too. He took a moment to marshal his voice.

'What are you doing here?'

'You need me.' Her tiny hands twisted in front of her, lost.

His pulse thundered. 'No, I don't. I'm getting by just fine.'

If 'fine' meant lying awake until he was too exhausted not to fall into a coma. And walking around this house as if he were a ghost, while everyone lived around him in a kind of parallel reality.

'I don't just mean now. I mean in life.' She took one forward step. 'You need me in your life.'

His enlarged heart pressed outwards on his ribcage until it threatened to crack.

'What's so special about you?' he fought. Hating himself, but hating this life his parents led more. Fearing it more than anything. Still disgusted with himself that he'd let it happen to him.

She wavered just the tiniest bit but then rallied. 'Last week

I would have struggled to answer that question, but I've had thirty hours and ten thousand miles to think about it.'

'And? What's your verdict?'

'I'm smart. And ethical. And kind. And loyal. But I'm far from perfect.'

He folded his arms tighter across his chest. If for no other reason than to hide his shaking fingers from her.

She'd already taken so much from him, she didn't get to have that as well.

Izzy crossed to look out of the floor-to-ceiling window onto his mother's extensive gardens, the Australian sun glowing clear through her pale dress. It silhouetted her body dramatically, until he had to move to the side of the room rather than let himself drown in memories of that lithe shape curled around him as they slept.

The last decent sleep he'd had.

'I broke my father's heart,' she started. 'The day he dropped me off at Trenton. I'd never seen him cry—ever—no matter how tough things got, financially, he always stayed strong. But he cried that day and I told myself it was just our parting but…it wasn't.' Her chest heaved. 'I think I broke his heart.'

She turned and paced back across the study, arms curled around her middle. 'He stood there, in front of our battered old car, and waved me off to the bright, new future I was so excited about. Me in my immaculate uniform that was the first new thing I'd ever worn. I couldn't have moved up those stone stairs faster. I didn't want anyone to see him or the car.'

Her sadness reached out and ebbed around his feet like London fog.

'You were a kid,' he defended before remembering he shouldn't.

'I rejected the life they'd struggled to give me. Like it wasn't good enough. And every time I called home with stories of the great experiences I was having at school I compounded the hurt. And I could hear that in their voices. So…I just…stopped calling. I started emailing. Sometimes texting. Eventually nothing.'

She trailed one absent finger along his father's desk.

'I traded my life for a new one,' she continued, voice rich with bitterness, 'and never looked back. Because it hurt too much, knowing what I'd done to my own parents. People I loved. Hearing it in their voices; knowing that they let me drop virtually out of their lives because they wanted me to be happy. And because I'd managed to make *them* feel ashamed about our life, too.'

She took a deep breath.

Her dignified pain reached out to him in a way he'd never experienced with anyone. All the deeper because she was trying so hard to mask it.

His feet started moving before he realised what was happening but he caught himself on the opposite side of the desk. Gripped the edge as if his survival depended on it.

'You flew halfway around the world to confess about your parents?'

She held his gaze. 'I let my relationship with my parents wither and die rather than acknowledge my shame at how I'd abandoned them, their love, our life, for a better offer. I adapted, I compensated and made sure I was always distracted from the thoughts. And life was okay. Like living without a limb. It can be done.'

'I don't understand.'

She stepped around the desk—floated really—and Harry's throat dried as he watched her.

'I know I can do it with you, too. Just…let you go. I'm really practised at it. It won't be easy but I'll compensate, adapt. And life will be okay again, afterwards.'

The finality of her serious speech infected him. And the meaning of her words coiled like a snake in his guts. 'Yet, here you are.'

'Because I don't *want* to let you go. Okay is no longer enough. I'm here to fight for what we had.'

'Izzy, what we had is over,' he gritted, more an affirmation for himself.

Her chest heaved in that insanely feminine dress. 'And what if I disagree?'

'Ending a relationship isn't usually mutual. Someone walks. It's over. That's how it works.'

Flies, in his case. First class. Not that he'd noticed one bit of the comfort.

A smile tickled at the edges of her lips. It did what it never failed to: made his heart squeeze. Except this time the squeezing hurt. Because he'd been so crazy about that smile.

'Yet, here I am,' she said.

He took a long, fortifying breath. Refusing to be manipulated. 'I'm sorry you wasted your time—' and presumably money she didn't have '—but nothing's changed from the last time we spoke.'

He turned and left the room. And it near killed him to leave her behind.

'One hour.'

After a week of whispers, Izzy's English alfresco voice fairly rattled through the big old house. He stalled. Turned. Stared. Because—dear God—he wanted that to be true. Even if he knew it didn't make any difference. He'd set his course now.

'One hour,' she repeated, dignified and strong. 'That's how long I'd known your secret when you left. Just one hour. And for most of that I was in a taxi trying to get to you.'

His breath lurched. But he'd been controlling his voice at management meetings way too long. He lifted one shoulder. 'So you say.'

'Name one time that I've lied to you.'

'How would I know?'

'I guess you wouldn't. I could be as good at it as you.' Her nostrils flared. 'Would it help if I offered witness statements?'

'Depends on the witnesses.'

'Poppy and Tori.'

'Those girls would die for you. I'm fairly sure they'd lie for you.'

'You really don't have a lot of faith in people, do you?'

Nope. He really didn't.

Apparently, with good cause.

She looked around the massive study, at the expensive art on the walls. She walked to one piece and stared at it for eternity. 'Is this where you grew up? This is normal to you?'

'I told you, I spent most of my time at boarding school.'

'But this is what waited for you when you came home?'

What the hell was she getting at now? 'Yes.'

'And your friends?'

'Of course, friends.'

'And girlfriends?'

'Izzy...'

'I remember how awed I was by Trenton. The trappings of wealth.'

She looked pretty awed by the art on the wall. A smile fought at the corners of his mouth. 'That's an original Mc-Cubbin. Hardly a trapping.'

She twisted back to him, nodding with interest, but it only took a moment for it to devolve into a scrunched nose. 'Actually, I don't care. I'm not much into art. I'm just being polite.'

Something silvery and wormlike twisted out of the black mass that was his heart and brought a lightness with it that he hadn't felt since London. But he fought it. Time to start winding this little reunion up. His patience was wearing thin and his resistance even thinner. He'd have to have her perfume scrubbed out of the walls as it was.

'Is that right?'

She ceased her exploration of the wall art and crossed to stand right in front of him.

'I can see why people might get dazzled by all this. Friends. Girlfriends.' She watched him closely. 'And how that might lead to some...bad situations for you.'

This close, he could see the evidence of the stresses of the past week much more clearly under her eyes. In the whiteness of her lips. He fought against the sense of triumph that she was doing as badly as he was. And not to care.

'Whereas you're entirely unmoved,' he guessed.

She glanced around again. 'It's not really to my taste,' she confessed.

'I don't think it's supposed to be to anyone's taste, Izzy. It's a statement of grandeur.'

'That statement being how much it cost?'

His snort echoed like a dog bark through the halls. '*Costs*, present tense. This estate costs a fortune every year to run.'

'Lucky you have several fortunes, then.'

Izzy's quick mind was no less sexy than when he'd first met her, and he began to remember exactly why he'd fallen for her. Words had been foreplay between them from the very beginning.

So he withheld any more.

'I had a lot of time to think after you left. Sitting there on the floor by your lift.'

The image of her, standing at his door, her slim hands reached out, beseeching, while he let a muscle-bound black-ops specialist physically push her away came back to him now.

Not his finest moment.

Where would all his sisters' pride be then?

He took her arm and turned her for the door and her practised composure finally slipped a little. As though his touch were all it took.

'Where are we going?' she gasped.

He knew where he was going for even entertaining a conversation with Izzy. *Masochism Central, population: one.*

'Somewhere more private.'

Izzy let herself be towed out into the bright spring sunlight and around the side of the house to a small sub-garden with hanging willows and perfectly positioned ornate benches. Very pretty. Very old.

Very easy to toss her from the property from here.

He released her and stood, arms folded, like a Roman centurion.

His fingers on her skin had just about broken her. The torment of his flesh on hers, but done with such icy calm. While her head was spinning with the right thing to say. To do.

Izzy struggled to clear her head, desperate not to be intimidated. Or at least not to show it.

'I called my mother after you left,' she started, again. 'I hated that my first proper call to them was because I needed something, but I really needed her. Her wisdom. Her composure. I needed someone who hadn't been charmed by your smile and wasn't influenced by having seen me so ridiculously delirious with you. I needed her clarity.' She curled her arms around her body. 'She suggested it might have been for the best, as unpleasant as our parting was. That I deserved better than someone who couldn't be honest with me, who couldn't share of themselves. Someone who could believe such a vile thing about me when I'd done nothing to earn that suspicion. Someone less damaged.'

The pulse at the angle of his jaw, that place she'd used to love to press her lips, worked visibly under his skin. Not reaching out to it took all her strength.

'I feel sure there's a point coming,' he said.

'Mum was right,' she gritted. 'But I couldn't get past what she'd said about damage. I couldn't help the suspicion that everything…all this we've been through…wasn't really about me, at all.'

She looked around her, at the expansive gardens, the grand old homestead. 'You must meet a lot of people who are very attracted to all this. People who are in it for the money. Now that I see it in context, it only reinforces what I was wondering.'

'And what's that?'

'Who it was that burned you so badly. That made you not trust anyone.'

His nostrils flared. 'You think I'm that oblivious? Or that careless with my assets? Especially my heart. In this family it pays to be guarded.'

Understanding blazed through her. 'You've never let someone in? You've never loved someone at all?'

Sorrow washed through her.

You never loved *me*.

'Bad investment,' he simply said. 'And I have too much uncertainty on my plate as it is. Love is a luxury I can't afford. I got slack. Forgot why people like us don't get to have ordinary lives.'

Oh, Harry… 'And that's why it was so easy for you to believe I'd been lying to you?'

'Look at it from my point of view, Izzy. *You* pursued *me*. Pitching Broadmore for funding, coming to my house, sliding so effortlessly into my life. And then I discover you knew who I was—'

'Just one hour, Harry.'

'One hour. One week. One month. In that moment, I felt…'

'Betrayed?' Yep, she knew that feeling. Like a hot knife between the ribs.

'I felt played.'

'But I didn't know.'

He shrugged. 'Maybe it was the wake-up call I needed. I was killing time in London, building up the experience I'd need to run Broadmore in the future. I wasn't there to make a life or fall in love. I'd lost sight of my purpose.'

'So you just…excised me?'

His eyes glittered. 'Why not? You did it to your parents.'

Ice-cold grief crystallised in her chest. Was this how they'd felt when she'd let them go? This awful…emptiness?

'My life was about to change anyway,' he urged. 'I was just pre-empting it. An emotional entanglement across the world from where my responsibilities were was exactly what I didn't need at that moment.'

Sudden pain curled like a fist in her throat.

Entanglement. Bound by twisted, clinging vines.

Right.

Izzy took a long, unsteady breath. She'd flown across the world on the off-chance that she could talk him around, once things were calmer, his father's condition stable. Once he'd heard her side of the story.

'I feared this would happen,' she murmured. 'That you'd

rationalise everything, file it away as a thing that happened once with a woman you knew for a few weeks. That you'd forget how good it felt being together. How perfect we were.'

'We dated for a few weeks, Izzy.' He shrugged, his eyes empty and hard. 'That's it.'

'I loved you for every one of those weeks,' she urged past the lump. 'Harry Mitchell, the man who blew his hard-earned wages on ferries and let me pluck the olives off his pizza and pledged to protect me when we walked at night.' Tears welled dangerously. 'And, I hunted for any kind of sign that you felt the same and cobbled together this stupid, misguided belief that you could care for someone like me.'

His throat worked visibly. 'How long would you have lasted in this world, anyway?'

If he'd given it half a chance? Maybe for ever.

But they'd never know now.

Izzy smoothed her dress and then stood as steadily as her physical and emotional exhaustion would allow. Her cold, dry palms were almost refreshing where the sun had just been.

'Because your world is so special, Harry? Doesn't really look it from here.'

She turned and took a few steps before pausing and turning back.

'For the record? *You* pursued *me*. You came to my house, seduced me in my bed, then again in yours, invited me to dinner and into your world. I wanted to trust you despite all the secrets and caginess—your mystery family, your clandestine past, your unspecified future. But you made me doubt what little you did tell me about yourself and, worse, you made me doubt myself. My worth.

'You kept yourself back from me like I meant nothing. But you also made love to me like I was a princess. And you looked at me like I was the centre of your world.

'And I believed your eyes.' She shuddered. 'Despite every fibre of my being warning me not to. Because I didn't want fear to keep me from letting myself love you. My inability to believe that poor little Isadora might have finally struck it rich, emotionally. I wanted to be braver than that.'

Those beautiful lips pressed flat across his jaw.

She turned and curled her hands around his arm, appealing to him.

'But my courage wasn't what I should have been worried about.'

His voice tightened. 'Don't worry about me, Izzy. I won't be single for long. The world is mine for the taking.'

Her jaw ached from clenching her back teeth. 'Something priceless was yours for the taking, Harry. All you had to do was believe in me.'

Her voice cracked entirely on those last words.

He cleared his throat but stood stiff and unrelenting. 'Do you need money for a taxi?'

Hurt surged along her bloodstream. That he thought a fistful of notes could buy her out of his life. Out of his conscience.

'I'm not interested in your money,' she said, stepping away from him. 'But thank you for reminding me it's there.'

CHAPTER THIRTEEN

'THERE'S SOME THINGS tea can't cure,' Izzy murmured towards the boxroom door that had crept open enough to let a stream of light into her darkness. She totally understood why wounded animals would find a log or a hole in the ground or in the rocks to curl up and die in. The closeness provided a strange kind of comfort.

Womb-like.

Tomb-like.

'Nonsense,' Poppy said, peering through. 'I'll never believe that.'

Izzy swung her legs over the edge of her bed and sat up slowly, gingerly receiving the piping-hot cuppa. Poppy's gentle smile was almost her undoing. 'Thank you.'

'How are you feeling?'

'Flat.'

'Well, flat is an improvement. Flat isn't sobbing.'

'Oh, I've had my quota of that today, too. And raging. And denial.'

Each one as futile as the others. Harry had made his mind up. The whole butterfly and tornado thing again.

'Why not come and sit out at the table?' Poppy implored, her dark eyes gently angled.

Poor Poppy. She had her own dramas to deal with and here she was having to babysit a hysterical flatmate. She, Tori and Alex had even taken it in turns to take a day off work to make sure she wasn't alone until next week when she was going home to Manchester and the gentle and accepting hands of her parents.

'Okay,' she sighed, and Poppy couldn't hide her relief. 'Yeah, okay.'

It might have been dinner time but it was still light out

and Izzy squinted in the rich evening light streaming in the windows.

All right, maybe she had been sequestered away a little too long.

Through the kitchen doorway, Alex stirred a large pot of something that made her empty stomach growl while Tori laid the living-room table. Business as usual. Except that Tori being here smacked of intervention.

She looked up. 'Hey, stranger.'

God, this was humiliating. Being the focus of so much pity. But only one person could change that.

'Anything I can do?' she offered, overly bright.

Poppy looked straight to Alex, who smiled and manufactured an impromptu task. 'Ah...I could use some help slicing the stir-fry.'

Okay. Stir-fry it was. She crossed to stand next to Alex in front of an array of market vegetables. 'Just thin sliced?'

'Nothing fancy.'

She took the chopping knife and began with the mushrooms. In her periphery, he kept a close eye on her. Very close.

'I'm not going to do anything drastic,' she confirmed.

'I'm more worried about me. The token male in the room. You could totally make it look like an accident.'

Hey, look at that; her lips still worked.

'Good to see you smile, Iz,' he murmured.

Sigh.

'Why are men so difficult to understand, Alex?'

If he only just caught on to what he'd signed up for when he found her a task, Alex hid it well. Or took it on like the warrior he was.

'We find you lot just as incomprehensible.'

She fell back to chopping and he fell back to stirring. Without looking, she could feel Poppy and Tori busying themselves with stay-close tasks.

He stepped aside and let her scrape the mushrooms into the vat of pasta sauce he was making before she reached for the peppers. But he paused and then turned to her, his voice low.

'Iz, this isn't about you. If he wanted to, he would have found some other way you failed him. No matter what you did.'

The thing about friends who said very little...you tended to listen very closely to what little they did say.

This isn't about you. Hadn't she come to much the same conclusion after all those long talks with her mother?

She nodded—just once—and lifted her eyes to her best friends, still hovering nearby on purposeless tasks: refolding the napkins and straightening the perfectly aligned cutlery. At all those familiar, beautiful faces. All staring at her. All full of concern.

'I love you guys,' she murmured. 'And I'm going to be okay. Tomorrow morning I'll start running again and I'll touch base with all my clients.'

Life could only pause for so long.

'Tomorrow's Saturday, Iz,' Tori reminded her gently.

Oh...right. Monday, then.

'Izzy, don't—' Poppy gnawed her lip.

'Don't what?'

She leaned forward intently. More focused than Izzy had seen her in a long time. 'Don't let this put you off. For ever, I mean. Harry was a good guy with some good qualities but he was just one man. You'll meet someone lovely who's able to be completely open with you and who sees you for who you really are. I promise. Please don't shut down emotionally.'

Someone lovely. That sounded so sweet and safe and... beige.

Someone lovely wasn't likely to twist her insides up tight enough to explode. Or make her weep with his touch. Or make her laugh out loud in public.

But, truth be told, a little emotional shut-eye sounded pretty good right now. It had been one hell of a fortnight.

She smiled tightly at the curious intensity in Poppy's eyes. Curious coming from a woman who hadn't been in a relationship since...ever.

'I hope you're right.'

'I am.'

But all of their faces said they heard the hollowness of Poppy's words, too. Alex excused himself and went into the kitchen to start dishing up.

'Knock knock?'

Izzy lifted heavy eyes to the doorway as a familiar face peered around it. Lara, from downstairs.

'I'm so sorry to interrupt,' she said. 'But there's a man down on the street who's trying to buzz your apartment but can't raise you. He's trying everyone in the building in rotation. I said I'd run up.'

'We muted it,' Poppy said, 'so we could have dinner.'

Lara flushed. 'Should I send him away, then?'

'Who is it?'

'Harry Mitchell. He's here for Izzy.'

Poppy's and Tori's gasps were perfectly synchronised.

'Harry?' Izzy croaked, her breath now firmly choked by the fist that had materialised in her chest.

'You don't have to, Iz,' Tori urged.

She turned towards two concerned faces. 'He's back.'

'You were just getting back on your feet,' Poppy muttered.

Her voice grew tiny and she turned her wide eyes to each of her oldest friends in turn. 'Why is he back, Toz?'

Tori shrugged her slim shoulders.

Lara cleared her throat, awkwardly, from the doorway. 'What would you like me to do?'

Poor girl. What an introduction. Izzy forced herself back to some semblance of normal.

'If you could let him into the building that would be super. Thank you!' she called as Lara disappeared back down the stairs to her small bedsit right below them.

She spun and looked straight to Tori, who knew, immediately, what she was asking.

'You look great.' But her eyes fell and her face followed suit. 'Although you have something on your sweatshirt.'

Tori turned and dashed into the boxroom, returning wearing a far less *lived-in* top.

I shouldn't care...I shouldn't care...

'What's going on?' Alex asked, emerging from the kitchen with the first two steaming bowls of pasta.

Poppy and Tori spun towards him but Izzy couldn't take her eyes off the door. Sure enough Harry stepped into it, puffing slightly from vaulting the stairs.

'You've got a bloody nerve—' Alex gunned straight for the front door.

Four female hands snagged him before he could get much past Izzy, and Harry skidded to a halt just outside the door.

Like a vampire that hadn't been invited in.

'Izzy,' he said, a whole lot of nothing in his eyes. Giving nothing away.

'Why are you here?'

'I wanted to speak to you.'

'We're in the middle of dinner.' What? Ridiculous. But her brain wasn't doing its finest work right now. 'You should have called.'

'I tried calling. Your phone's been going straight to voice mail since yesterday.'

Oh.

'The battery died.' Sometime during her self-imposed sequester. Something to do with listening to his 'I love you' voice mail over and over.

Ad nauseam.

'You'll have a bunch of missed calls from me when you charge it up. Tracking my progress from Melbourne airport.'

The silence that fell was punctuated only by the three sets of heavy breathing behind her.

Well...wasn't this nice?

'How's your father?' she asked past her tight throat.

'Getting there.' He glanced over her shoulder and then back. 'Can I...? Can we speak, privately?'

'This is their home, too.' And she absolutely wasn't having any kind of conversation with him in the boxroom. It was hard enough getting to sleep now, without it filling with his particular scent.

'A walk, then?'

'I'll need a second.'

'Okay.'

Izzy walked, numb but steady, to her room and then to the bathroom, where she pulled on a jumper, combed her hair and brushed her fuzzy teeth. She gargled for good measure.

Deluded optimist.

But if Harry was here as part of some extended farewell tour, she wasn't having his last memory being her looking like road-kill. She'd prefer to be remembered as the one that got away.

Actually she'd prefer to be the one-that-got-to-stay but that wasn't happening any time soon.

When she re-emerged, the tension in their flat was richer than the colour scheme. Harry busily ignored the three sets of death stare blazing at him and kept his eyes tracked on the door she'd disappeared through.

At the slightest noise from her Alex, Tori and Poppy all spun around.

'You don't have to do this, Iz,' Alex gritted. 'I can make him leave.'

No doubt, given his background. But given Harry's martial arts training one or both of them would end up hurt. She squeezed Alex's arm and smiled at her girlfriends.

'It's okay. I'll be back in a while. I could use the air, anyway.'

Concern ran ahead of them and tangled in her feet as she crossed to follow Harry back down the stairs. They descended in silence and didn't speak until they were out on the street.

Three gazes practically burned into the back of Izzy's head from the upstairs window.

'I didn't expect to see you—' ever again '—back in London.'

'I had to wind things up at Broadmore Natále and hand over to my replacement.'

Ironic since that was the lie she'd told to get into his house in Australia. She led him around the corner to a park play-ground on the next street.

'I thought you'd have people to do that for you, now that you're the big cheese. Or Skype or something.'

'Some things you can't outsource.'

She steered them into the park and turned to face him. To stare into those beautiful eyes. Just stare. He'd come to her. The next step had to be his.

He composed himself, visibly, and then started speaking. Formally, as if he'd been practising on the plane. Turmoil boiled behind his eyes. But it coalesced into a kind of certainty.

And she knew he was finally going to be honest.

'Just over five years ago, my father paid someone a fortune to bring a heap of old family documents into Broadmore's content management system, and a letter *about* me was mis-filed as being *to* me. It showed that my school captaincy—an honour I believed I'd earned—was in return for spanking new science-lab equipment my father donated. The more I dug, the more coincidental donations I discovered. My academic achievements. Jiu-jitsu awards…'

Five years. Right about when he changed his name and left Australia for Britain.

'Every girlfriend I had growing up was with me for the lifestyle that a rich young kid could provide. I picked girls who were friends with my sisters because I assumed they'd be less dazzled by the money. But it turns out many of their parents were encouraging them to befriend my sisters as a way to get closer to the future CEO of Broadmore Consolidated. But when they eventually went their way—and they always did—it wounded me *and* whatever sister they'd used to get to me. And I realised I was hurting my sisters.

'So I changed my approach as soon as I hit uni. I stuck to women where we both knew the score. No betrayals, no innocent façades. I spent on them generously and publicly. They were openly in it for the reward and…I guess so was I.'

'Those must have been cynical, lonely years,' she murmured, hating the idea of anyone touching him before her.

He shrugged. 'It was safer and it kept my family out of it. And if I felt myself growing connected to one of the women, all I had to do was tighten the flow of money and I'd get an instant reminder of why they were really there.'

'None of them cared for you? At all?'

What was wrong with Australian women? How could they know him and not love him?

'They all delighted in having a healthy young man to break in. But that wasn't why they were there. And I can't blame them. I set the rules. But it wasn't enough. I needed to know who *I* was...on my own.'

'So you became Harry Mitchell.'

'And I got an entry-level job in my father's company without him knowing and then worked my way up. He eventually cottoned on. It amused him to watch my progress, at first, but then he saw how settled I was getting here and so he turned on the screws, reminding me of my obligations, and me staying became conditional on us both considering it in-house training.

'I got another promotion and I really started to wonder whether he was orchestrating those, as well. So I began testing people. Seeing if I could get away with murder. Seeing who'd just wear it.'

'And who did?'

'One or two. But not a bolshy, blonde finance officer who was assigned to me fourteen months ago. She gave me no quarter at all.'

'That explains your management approach, then...'

'Izzy, everything I've ever achieved has been because of my name, my family, the bank balance that would some day be mine,' he started. 'I wanted to see what I could achieve without any of those things behind me.'

He shuffled around, more face-on. 'And I achieved *you,* Iz. Quirky, high-maintenance and left-of-centre you. This gorgeous woman who I'd lusted after for a year, who came to be interested in a snarky finance manager whose only redeeming quality was his circus skills in the sack. And I was really happy with that. Because you'd chosen *Harry Mitchell*. On his own merits, not because of a name.

'But then you thought I hadn't.'

'I didn't want to know how long you'd known my secret, because I was scared of the answer. Scared of hearing you say it. But I should have known, I should have believed you. Or done just about anything other than shouting at you and leaving the country before you could defend yourself. My head was just so…compressed with memories and images, which all looked totally different through a darker filter.'

'It was a rough time—'

'I was raised to push through rough times. And I knew my old man was too much of a control freak to actually die.' He shook his head. 'I have no excuse for the conclusions I jumped to. At least I didn't think I did. But then you turned up at my house.'

He said that as if it were the most audacious and awe-inspiring thing he'd ever heard of. As if no one ever just *turned up*.

'You fronted me on my own turf, and you stood there all beautiful and fresh and *honest* and, after you'd gone, that impression wouldn't leave me. And all those memories and images started to replay again through a different filter. A blindingly bright one.'

He took her hand.

'They were completely changed, Iz. Genuine. Unpolluted. The way I'd experienced them the first time. I realised, then, that I'd fixated on the fact that you'd known rather than on the fact that you were one of two people in the world I *could have* trusted with the information. That I *should* have.'

'Why didn't you?'

He slumped down onto the playground see-saw and straddled it. She stepped quietly around to its opposite. When it had completely stilled from its bouncy adjustment, he resumed speaking.

'My mother wasn't even twenty when she started working at Broadmore's Melbourne office and met my father. I
wouldn't be surprised if she hadn't sought a job there purely
to meet him. She was pretty motivated. I don't know what
she did to hypnotise him or whether the realities of marriage
were just too mundane but, the moment the ink was dry on
their nuptial agreement, all that allure just fell away. And all
they were left with was the husk of a not very deep, not very
long, not very good relationship.'

Izzy frowned. 'They brought four kids into that family.'

'Part of the agreement. He wanted an heir.'

'Oh, Harry...'

'It hurts kids to grow up like that, Iz,' he breathed. 'My
sisters are as messed up as I am in their own ways. But I sat
there and sucked in the veiled looks through osmosis; the
snarky comments, the telephone conversations to friends and
lovers they probably thought I couldn't hear or understand.
I watched my father—a man I wanted to love and respect—
paying the lifetime price for his weakness about this woman,
and I watched her enjoy a string of relationships with people
other than my father, loving them, and then brushing them
off when they ended, and finding someone new.

'But, as I grew, I realised her love for *them* was virtually
indistinguishable from her love for *me*,' he said. 'And she told
the world she loved my father but really she can barely tolerate him. So how could our love be any realer?'

The pain in her chest—the one that had finally eased off
following her return from Australia—surged back now, angry
and tight.

Her fingers itched to find his.

So this was why he protected his heart?

'And so I grew up believing that love was just a thing you
said for effect or put on for show, like the flash entry hall of
my house. It was where you stood your sculptures or hung
your expensive art or custom-woven drapes. It was a trapping
of success. It didn't have to be real.

'But I hadn't realised until I was standing in my doorway

shouting at your pale, devastated face what that had done to me. What it had made me.'

He leaned forward and snared her gaze with his.

'I'm here for two reasons and the first is to beg your forgiveness, Izzy, for the way I spoke to you. Here and in Australia.'

'Do you believe I wasn't faking it?'

'Absolutely.'

'Do you trust me?'

'Yes.'

'You paused.'

He ran his fingers through his hair. 'It doesn't come naturally, Izzy. It's going to take a little work.'

The future tense had her breath coiling up all over again in her chest. 'Why couldn't you tell me your secrets?'

'I was so smitten with you. So distracted and glassy-eyed. We went tumbling past the point at which telling you would have been natural.'

Tumbling into bed, knowing them.

'And then I'd left it too long. It got harder every day I left it.'

Just like her parents.

'But you'd been so great about it, so relaxed and undemanding, and I treasured that after the women I'd had in my life.'

'I was waiting stoically for you to tell me,' she murmured.

He forked his fingers through his hair. 'I recognise that now.'

'Long way to fly to apologise.'

'In my message on the day of Dad's heart attack, I said there was something I wanted to tell you. This was it. I was going to tell you everything—all of it. Back then.'

Until she'd gone tearing over like a banshee with all her support and kindness.

'That's not all you said.'

'No.' He stood slowly so that her end of the see-saw didn't dump her off. Then he drew her back to her feet, too. 'And it killed me that the first time I said it was in a voice mail. That's not how I'd imagined saying those words.'

She tried to smile, but suspected she wasn't pulling it off. 'Not really how I'd imagined hearing them.'

'In my message I also said I had something to give you. I had it on me that day. I've kept it with me since we last saw each other.'

He rummaged in the pocket of his long coat and presented her with a small, soft toy.

She stared at it. 'A platypus?'

'It was the closest I could find to an otter at Melbourne airport. I've been clutching that since Australia. Had to fight a four-year-old for it.'

She blinked back at him.

'Turn it over, Izzy.'

She did, and he looked pointedly at the suspiciously pouch-like recess at its fluffy belly.

Something glinted back at her from deep inside.

She lifted her eyes to Harry's, all breath suspended, and half whispered, 'What are you doing?'

'Something I should have done back when I first bought it.'

Back...?

'And when was that?' she asked, carefully.

'The morning of my father's heart attack.'

Every part of her wanted to weep. For the loss, if it was true. For the cruelty of saying it, if it was not. But she wiggled the ring free of its furry prison and turned it over gently in her fingers, her heart pounding.

White gold. Simple and unpretentious.

The squeeze morphed into an almost unbearable ache. 'And you think an expensive parting gift is going to make things right between us?'

Case in point, really. Their whole dysfunctional relation-ship in a single painful, pricey gesture.

'It's not a parting gift.' His lips twisted. 'And it wasn't that expensive.'

She ignored the first part on pure self-defence grounds.

'Aren't you going to ask me why I bought you a ring, Izzy?'

No. Because her wounded heart was already in fibrilla-tion. How much more could she expect it to take? She shook her head—barely.

'I wanted something to celebrate our thirtieth date. I wanted something to celebrate the crazy connection we had and the fact we'd spent every night for four weeks together. I got it because as I stood there holding that bloody ring, I could practically feel it on your fingers as they curled in mine and it just felt…so right.'

His eyes moistened a hint. 'I got it for you, Izzy.'

'Thirty dates?'

'That's what I told myself when I went in the store.'

'And when you came out?'

'Look at it. It's hardly a friendship ring, is it?'

Staring down at it only highlighted how badly her hands were shaking. She curled them around the ring.

'I'd planned to propose, Izzy.'

Rip.

There it went. Her heart's last defences. Pain washed along every artery and vein in her body.

'In case I hadn't already realised how much I'd lost?' she choked. 'That's why you're telling me now?'

He stepped right up to her. Curled his hands over hers.

'I'm telling you because I overreacted, Iz. Because I let my screwed-up idea of what love is grow like a tumour, and I put that before everything else. I came home from buying that for you to an urgent call from my sister and spent all af-ternoon on the phone long distance to an uncommunicative hospital, and the whole time, instead of worrying about my family, all I could feel was this crushing sensation, squeez-ing in from outside.' He stepped closer. 'That I'd have to go home. That I'd have to leave you.

'I thought my life was over in that moment, Iz. And in that same moment I realised that what you and I had together *had become* my life. Everything I needed. All I wanted. And I immediately started thinking about how I could have both.

Desperate, anxious thinking. I'm sure you heard it in my voice on the message.'

Had she? All she'd heard was someone desperate to get off the phone. Or maybe she'd had her own dark filter on.

Her eyes trailed all over his face. Every anxious line, every pinched nerve. And something compelled her to keep this unexpected line of honesty between them open.

'You can't have both.'

'I can. I will.'

'Then what will happen with the company?'

'I'm going to run it.'

'A massive commitment.'

'Fortunately for me I'm not quite as much of a dinosaur as my father,' he said. 'I have an extremely talented and extremely willing older sister who has been proving herself for twenty years now. Carla was more than happy to take over our operations in Australasia.'

The turn screws holding her lungs in place cranked around a few times more and her breath struggled for passage. 'And what about you?'

'I'll handle Europe and North America.'

Every bit of saliva decamped from her mouth. 'Where will you be based?'

His whole face softened on a smile. 'Our London offices.'

She took three long, deep breaths. 'So you're back until...?'

Finishing the sentence herself was just too risky. Her voice was going to crack.

'Until you tell me to leave.'

Every part of her wanted to dance around the park. Even though she didn't yet have a right to.

'And this ring is...?'

'The ring is yours, if you'll take it.'

She clutched the little platypus in one hand and Harry's ring in the other. Then she handed it back to him.

'I feel like I barely know you again.'

His face fell. 'You don't want it?'

'Taking it doesn't seem right. After everything we've been through. Not now.'

Blue eyes bled the loss. 'Have I wrecked everything, Iz?'

Had he? Technically he hadn't proposed but he'd meant to, before everything went so badly wrong. And would she have said yes? Maybe. Except that everything she'd discovered, everything she'd seen in Australia, made it clear just how different their worlds were.

'I'm not interested in your money, Harry.'

Confusion stained his gaze. 'I know.'

'I'm actually quite intimidated by it. You said yourself that I might not even fit in your world. What if that's true?'

'Then we'll create our own world. Our own place, our own rules. Whatever we want it to be.'

'I'm not really CEO-wife material.' The old doubt demons danced around her heart.

'Then don't marry Harrison Broadmore. Marry Harry Mitchell.'

He took both her hands in his and Izzy realised how desperately she'd been wanting to touch him. She curled her fingers into his and held on.

'How about this…?'

His eyes flicked around as he desperately thought something through, and they fell on the platypus-that-should-have-been-an-otter. 'Let's redo the first thirty dates. Thirty dates based on nothing less than full and total disclosure. And during that time the ring stays in the otter-pus.'

He took the ring and tucked it safely back into the toy pouch and then curled her hands over it.

'And thirty dates from now we sit down in our living room, in front of all of London, and I'm going to give you this ring again. Properly, on bended knee and everything, and only *then* will I accept a no from you, Isadora Dean. Because, despite what an abomination I made of this whole thing, I can't breathe when I think about how long and empty my life will be without you in it. Easily as miserable as my parents'.'

He shuffled in closer and framed her face. 'You were right,

Izzy. I do need you, desperately. Who else will give me grief and keep me humble when the rest of the world is sucking up? I don't need or want anyone else by my side, in my bed or in my head. Only you.'

She swallowed past the words that had tumbled and fallen in a heap in her airway.

'I love you, Isadora Dean. And thirty dates' worth of patience is nothing compared to the lifetime I want to have with you.'

Maybe there was still some life in her poor heart yet. It lurched back to regular rhythm and then fluttered up to a breath-stealing gallop. She met Harry's mouth halfway down to her and locked her lonely, wasted lips on his, and knew that was where they belonged.

They always had.

He tasted and smelled and felt exactly the same.

Like home.

Like for ever.

She tore her mouth free as his words soaked through her clouded, joyous mind. '*Our* living room?'

'You don't imagine I'm going to waste a moment of those thirty dates on public transport, do you? I want you with me, close to me, twenty-four-seven. I want to fall asleep with you wrapped around me and I want to wake up to you still there. I want to eat fish and chips with you on the carpet looking over London, and I want to watch you spending a whole week building up to a big night out.'

The scars on her heart flexed and loosened up.

'We've not even been on a date yet. I might not be that easy.'

'You slept with me before our other first date, if I recall. That's how easy you were.'

'I was impatient. And maybe a little bit drunk.'

'I pledge to keep you that way always. Move in with me, Iz? Straight away.'

'I'm supposed to be going to my parents' next week. I can't let them down. They've been so generous. So forgiving.'

'I'll come with you. I figure I owe them as much of an explanation as you.'

'And the girls… They both want to kill you.'

'I'll stand and take my hits like a man. Even from Alex.'

Pfff. 'Who do you think fronted me the grand to fly to Australia?' she said. 'Alex considers himself a stakeholder in our relationship. He'll be thrilled you're back.'

Hot lips found hers again.

'And what happens if I say no in thirty days' time?' she breathed. 'I won't have a room to go back to.'

'You're not going to say no. We're meant to be together. But if you don't want the ring, then, I'll move out and you can stay in the Vauxhall apartment until something else comes up. You have my word.'

She snorted against the tears. 'You have way too much money, Harry Mitchell Broadmore.'

'And I'll love watching you try not to spend it, Isadora Broadmore.' He presented her with the otter-pus again. 'So what do you say? Want to give it a try?'

She took it, found herself utterly unable to let go of it at all, and her pinkie snagged the ring out into the evening light. 'I don't think an otter-pus should be trusted with something this important,' she murmured, staring at the simple, sparkling beauty of it. Wanting—desperately—to feel it on her finger.

'I guess a few more weeks in my pocket won't hurt it.'

Izzy shied away from his questing fingers, holding on to the ring. 'Or…I could wear it. See how I feel about it.'

'You don't think an engagement ring is going to draw unhelpful attention?'

'I'll wear it on my right hand—' and only occasionally swap it to her left '—no one will notice it amongst my other jewellery.'

Except that she never wore rings. And Poppy and Tori were *totally* going to notice.

'Here, let me.'

Harry twisted sideways and took her right hand, then slid

it on next to the pinkie finger that had just fished it out of the otter-pus's belly.

'Isadora Dean,' he said, his beautiful blue eyes locked on hers. 'Will you think about being my wife, approximately thirty days from now?'

Maybe neither of them was going to say it aloud but there was no question.

Harry was proposing...and Izzy was saying yes.

She smiled. 'I'll get back to you.'

'Good enough.'

And, for what followed, Izzy was grateful that this little pocket park was as quiet as it was. And that the shadows were lengthening. Harry kissed her as if they were alone in his massive bed.

'I should get back and start packing, then,' she gasped, finally lifting her head.

Harry grimaced, pulling her to her feet and smoothing down her mismatched outfit. 'They're not going to be happy I'm stealing you away,' he said.

'Poppy and Tori are going to be bridesmaids. All will be forgiven.'

The one thing she could count on was her friends backing her choices one hundred per cent. No matter what.

'Especially when I fly them out to Australia for our second ceremony.'

Her eyebrows shot up. 'We're having two weddings?'

'A modest Izzy-appropriate one here, and a lavish heir-appropriate one back home. You can meet my sisters.'

'I'd really like that,' she murmured, curling the fingers of her right hand through his. His eyes fell to where they joined and lingered.

'Does it feel like you imagined?'

'Just like it. A perfect fit.'

That ring belonged on her finger, and her fingers belonged threaded through his.

They strolled back towards the fire station, taking their time, remembering how it felt to brush against each other.

How the sparks still flew whenever they touched. How much they'd missed it.

'One last thing, Harry.' Izzy smiled up at him.

'What, beautiful?'

'I may be bringing a few things with me,' she mused. 'How big is your boxroom?'

* * * * *

If you loved this book, make sure you catch
the rest of the incredible
THE FLAT IN NOTTING HILL *miniseries!*

THE MORNING AFTER THE NIGHT BEFORE
by Nikki Logan, available August 2014
SLEEPING WITH THE SOLDIER
by Charlotte Phillips, available September 2014
YOUR BED OR MINE?
by Joss Wood, available October 2014
ENEMIES WITH BENEFITS
by Louisa George, available November 2014